DANGEROUS WATERS

SANDRA ROBBINS

HARLEQUIN LOVE INSPIRED® SUSPENSE

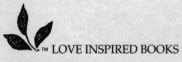

™ LOVE INSPIRED BOOKS

Recycling programs
for this product may
not exist in your area.

ISBN-13: 978-0-373-44550-9

DANGEROUS WATERS

www.LoveInspiredBooks.com

Printed in U.S.A.

Laura cast one last terrified glance around the parking lot and took a deep breath. "We've got to get out of here. They're watching us."

Brad's frown deepened. "Who's watching us?"

"The man who abducted me last night. He knew I'd been to the police, and he knew what I was wearing."

Brad steered her back toward the car. "Get in the car, Laura. I need to get you out of here."

Once inside he cranked the engine and roared from the parking lot. As he sped down the street, he looked in the rearview mirror from time to time. "I don't think we're being followed. I don't know who these guys are, but we'll do our best to find out. Until we do, I want you to lie low, and let us do our job."

She stared out the window without answering him. For years she had convinced herself she could live with the unanswered questions about her parents' deaths, but now she knew that was impossible.

The events of last night and today had propelled her past a point of no return, and now she wouldn't give up until she had the answers she'd craved.

Books by Sandra Robbins

Love Inspired Suspense

Final Warning
Mountain Peril
Yuletide Defender
Dangerous Reunion
Shattered Identity
Fatal Disclosure
*Dangerous Waters

*The Cold Case Files

SANDRA ROBBINS,

a former teacher and principal in the Tennessee public schools, is a full-time writer for the Christian market. She is married to her college sweetheart, and they have four children and five grandchildren. As a child, Sandra accepted Jesus as her Savior and has depended on Him to guide her throughout her life.

While working as a principal, Sandra came in contact with many individuals who were so burdened with problems that they found it difficult to function in their everyday lives. Her writing ministry grew out of the need for hope that she saw in the lives of those around her.

It is her prayer that God will use her words to plant seeds of hope in the lives of her readers. Her greatest desire is that many will come to know the peace she draws from her life verse, Isaiah 40:31. "But those who hope in the Lord will renew their strength. They will soar on wings like eagles; they will run and not grow weary; they will walk and not be faint."

But I will hope continually,
and will yet praise thee more and more.
—*Psalms* 71:14

To my sisters Pam, Fran and Sandy
for all your encouragement and support

ONE

Even though Laura Webber had watched the prerecorded television interview on the six o'clock news, she couldn't wait to see the repeat at ten. She'd spent the time between the broadcasts finishing up paperwork in her office at the hospital, and then switched on the television to catch it again on the late news. She stared at her pale face on the screen and wondered how her friend and roommate, Grace Kincaid, had ever talked her into doing that interview.

She'd promised herself when she'd returned to Memphis she wouldn't dredge up the memories she'd lived with for the past nineteen years. And yet, there she was on the most watched television station in the city telling how her parents had died in a car bomb explosion when she was ten years old.

Grace, ever the professional reporter, stared into the camera to close the interview. "The deaths of Lawrence Webber and his wife, Madeline, are one of the many unsolved cases that have prompted local authorities to establish a new Cold Case unit within the police department. The Webbers are but one family who hopes they will soon have answers concerning the fates of their loved ones. I am Grace Kincaid reporting for WKIZ-TV. Thank you for watching."

Laura pressed the remote to switch off the television, leaned forward and folded her arms on her desk. At first she hadn't wanted to do the interview. The memory of seeing the car bomb explode and engulf her parents in flames still haunted her. Grace had reasoned with her that people needed to be reminded that a federal prosecutor and his wife had been murdered while his children watched, and she was right. It felt good to know she had told her parents' story.

She glanced at the clock and jumped to her feet. Time to get home. If she was to make it to her early appointments with clients at Cornerstone Clinic in the morning, she needed some sleep. She grabbed her purse hanging on the back of her chair and slid its strap over her shoulder. A chill rippled down her spine as a thought flashed in her mind. The next hospital shift wouldn't occur for another hour. The parking lot would be deserted this late.

Her chin dipped against her chest, and she covered her face with her hands. Through the years she'd thought of what she'd lost that summer day years ago when her parents' car exploded, but it was what she'd gained that kept her awake at nights—the fear that someone was watching her and her brother, just waiting for the chance to annihilate her entire family.

After a moment, she took a deep breath, switched off her office lights and headed for the parking lot. Before stepping outside the hospital, she peered through the door's glass at the dark shadows covering the asphalt beyond the exit. Several streetlights appeared to be out of order. She squinted into the distance trying to remember where she'd parked her car. With the lot filled when she arrived earlier this afternoon, she hadn't been able to get her spot near the building. Scanning the area, she finally spotted her vehicle underneath one of the poles that burned brightly. The distance between where she stood and her car seemed to grow as she stared at it. After a moment she squared her shoulders, stepped from the building and walked toward her car. Her gaze didn't waver as she moved.

Halfway to her destination, the sound of a car door closing echoed across the parking lot, and she froze in place. She cast a glance around but didn't see anyone. A footstep echoed off the asphalt. Was it her imagination, or was someone out there?

She dug in her purse for her keys as she bolted toward her car. Without warning an arm circled her waist and squeezed the breath from her. A hand clamped a cloth over her mouth and nose, blocking the scream rising in her throat. Twisting and kicking, she tried to loosen her attacker's grip, but it was no use. Dizziness swept over her, and she struggled against it. But there was nothing to ward off the darkness that enveloped her.

Disoriented, she awoke with a start. Where was she? How long had she been out? She strained to catch a glimpse of something in the inky darkness that surrounded her, but she could see nothing. She blinked, and her eyelashes brushed against something.

She lay on her side, her arms behind her back. With a tug, she tried to pull her hands to her chest, but something cut into her wrists. She moaned in pain as the truth began to seep into her head. She couldn't see because a blindfold covered her eyes, and she couldn't move because her hands were tied behind her back.

What had happened? Bits and pieces of memory trickled into her brain. The hospital—she had left after watching the interview on TV and walked toward her car. But she didn't recall getting in it.

Then she remembered a cloth over her nose, a man's arm around her waist. Fear rose in her throat. She had broken the first rule she gave crime victims in her counseling sessions—always be mindful of your surroundings. But she hadn't been. Not until it was too late.

Now she lay blindfolded and bound somewhere. She stilled and listened for any clue that might give a hint of her surroundings. The steady hum of an engine and the slapping of tires on pavement answered her question. She was in some kind of vehicle heading toward an unknown destination.

She strained to pull her hands free, but it was no use. Her head jerked at the sharp slap to her face. "It's no use, Laura," a man's voice whispered in her ear. "You can't get loose."

The smell of tobacco and alcohol assaulted her nostrils and she gagged. Then cold fear shot through her veins. He knew her name. This was no random abduction. It was personal.

"Wh-what do you want with me?" Her dry throat burned so that the words were barely more than a whisper.

"I want to talk to you about your television interview."

Her heart pounded, and she tried to swallow but her mouth had gone dry. "Wh-what about it?"

Something sharp nicked the skin beneath her chin. Laura tried to pull back from the knife's tip, but the man pressed it closer. "Some people I know don't want you talking about what happened. They think it's better to bury the past. What do you think?"

Tears rolled down her face. "What are you going to do to me?"

He laughed, and the sound sent chill bumps down her spine. "I'm going to make sure you don't talk to anybody else about that car bomb that killed your parents. Your search for answers is going to stop tonight. Understand?"

There was no denying what his words insinuated. He intended to kill her. Her body shook, but she pushed back the groans that rumbled in her throat. The vehicle came to a stop, and another man's voice cut through the silence. "We're here. Get it over with quick."

Before she realized what was happening, she was jerked from the vehicle and stood upright. A man's hand grasped her upper arm so tightly she thought it might cut off her circulation. He reached behind and yanked the ties from her around her hands. She pulled her hands up and rubbed her wrists.

Her knees threatened to collapse at the nudge of a gun against her back. "Now walk forward," he muttered. "And don't look back. Just walk."

"P-please," she begged.

"Walk," he snarled and pushed her forward.

Laura took a hesitant step and then another. Cold water seeped through the soles of her shoes, but she stumbled on. Her heart beat faster every time she moved. Would this step be her last?

A sound like water lapping against a shore reached

her ears, and she shuddered at the familiar sound. He had brought her to the bank of the Mississippi River. Now she understood. A shot in the back, and her body would float downriver toward the Gulf of Mexico and never be seen again.

She clenched her fists and thought of her brother, Mark, his wife, Betsy, and their new daughter, Amanda, on Ocracoke Island. She'd never see them again. "God," she whispered, "watch over my family. Don't let them grieve for me."

Cold water rolled over her feet, and she hesitated. "Keep walking," the voice yelled.

She took another step and knew she now stood in the river. She inched forward until the water reached her knees, but the shot still didn't come. Suddenly a motor cranked and tires squealed. She held her breath and waited, but nothing happened.

With shaking hands she reached up, pulled the blindfold from her eyes and turned to stare to her left. The lights of Memphis blinked in the distance. The bridge that connected the city to Arkansas lit the night, and she could see cars whizzing along its roadway. It only took her a moment to figure out that she'd been brought to the northern end of Mud Island.

She turned slowly and stared behind her. There was no one there, and no vehicle sat at the side of the road. With tears streaming down her face she waded out of the water and collapsed on her hands and knees on the riverbank. A combination of fear and relief surged through her body, and she gulped great breaths of air into her lungs.

The melody of "Can't Help Falling in Love," her favorite Elvis song and the ringtone on her cell phone, pierced the darkness. She stumbled to her feet and headed toward the sound. Her purse lay in the grass about ten feet from the water's edge.

She pulled her phone from the purse and rammed it to her ear. "Hello?"

The voice that had chilled her in the vehicle drifted into her ear. "This was a warning, Laura. Let the past go, or next time you won't be so lucky." She cringed at the evil chuckle ringing in her ear. "Be sure and check the local news in the morning. They say history repeats itself. Just make sure it doesn't happen to you, too."

The caller disconnected. Laura pulled the phone from her ear and stared at it. After a moment she sank to her knees again, wrapped her arms around her waist and wailed until she was exhausted. Then she pushed to her feet and began to walk toward the lights of Memphis.

Brad Austin yawned and rubbed the back of his neck as he strode down the hall at police headquarters. He'd been up all night, and he was exhausted. But there was no time to rest. He hadn't thought this job as one of the detectives heading the new Cold Case unit would be as demanding as his former detective job, but so far it had kept him even busier.

He glanced at his watch and frowned. 7:00 a.m. He'd been at the hospital since eleven last night. If Seth and Alex, his partners, were in the office, he'd bring them up to speed on the Nathan Carson lead before he headed back to either the hospital or to the medical examiner's office, depending on whether Carson lived or died.

As Brad walked past the break room, he smelled

coffee. That's what he needed right now. He stepped inside, poured himself a cup and sipped the hot liquid as he thought back over the events of the past few days.

Three days ago he'd received a telephone call from a man who identified himself as Nathan Carson, long-time accountant for a local crime family headed by Tony Lynch. Brad had been interested immediately because every cop in town wanted to take down the Lynch organization. Now with Tony retired and living in Florida, a new leader had risen from the ranks, but so far his identity had remained a secret.

At first Brad had been skeptical, but when Carson offered to identify the new leader of the family, he became interested. In addition, Carson also claimed to have information about the five-year-old cold case of a murdered undercover policeman for the Drug Task Force found on the banks of the Mississippi River in Memphis. He hinted at knowing what the officer had discovered shortly before he was killed. That statement had been enough to convince Brad this could be the lead he'd been waiting for.

Only the police and the FBI who'd been called in after the murder knew about the officer's last message to his superiors before his death. He'd discovered that drugs were but one of the Lynch family's businesses. Another was the transportation and sale of illegal aliens along the Mississippi.

Carson had promised to meet with Brad at his office today. That wasn't going to happen now because Nathan Carson's car had exploded in a ball of flames last night when he'd turned the ignition in the parking garage of the office building where he worked. Now he fought for his life in one of the city's best trauma units.

Brad narrowed his eyes and shook his head. He didn't believe in coincidences. What were the odds that two cold cases with suspected ties to the Lynch organization could be connected by a car bomb? The bomb squad had the remains of last night's bomb right now, and he could hardly wait to find out if it bore any resemblance to the one that had killed federal prosecutor Lawrence Webber and his wife nineteen years ago.

That case was another of the files that had been turned over to him when he'd taken this new job, and for personal reasons he'd like to see it solved more than any other. He drained the last drop of his coffee and threw the disposable cup in the trash before he headed down the hall.

As he approached his office, a uniformed officer stepped out and closed the door. "Good morning, Officer Johnson," Brad said. "What can I do for you this morning?"

The man jerked his thumb toward the closed door. "Late last night patrol picked up a woman they spotted walking from the direction of the boat ramp on Mud Island. They brought her to the station, but she insisted she could only talk to you. I just left her in your office."

"What she was doing out there alone late at night?"

The officer shook his head. "I have no idea. Wouldn't tell us a thing except she had information about one of your cold cases." He glanced down at his watch. "I'm off duty, and I'm ready to go home."

"I wish I could go home," Brad said with a sigh. "But it looks like my day is off to a good start. Are Seth and Alex in yet?"

"Didn't see 'em."

"Well, thanks for bringing the woman down here. I'll see what she wants."

Brad opened the door and stepped into the office. The woman sat slumped over the desk in his cubicle. Her head was buried in her crossed arms on top of the desk, and she didn't stir as he closed the door. She appeared to be sound asleep.

He cleared his throat, but she didn't move. He waited a moment before he crossed to where she sat and stopped beside her. "May I help you?" he asked.

A soft snore was the only response he received.

Brad grasped her shoulder and gave a gentle shake. "May I help you?" he repeated in a louder voice.

A scream tore from her mouth, and she jumped to her feet. She recoiled against the desk and stared at him with wild eyes. Then she relaxed and let out a long breath. "Oh, thank goodness, it's you, Brad."

He opened his mouth, but no words came out. He winced at the pain in his stomach that felt as if he'd been kicked. It couldn't be. Laura? What was she doing in his office?

His heart beat so hard he feared it might jump out of his chest. He staggered backward a step and shook his head. "I can't believe it. What are you doing here?"

Her brow drew into a weary frown, and she rubbed her hands over her eyes. "I know you're shocked to see me, but after what happened to me last night, I had to see you."

For a moment all he could do was stare in shock at her, then his gaze drifted over her body. Her red eyes and the way she sagged against the desk suggested she was near exhaustion. Dried mud caked the pants and top of the blue scrubs she wore, and her shoes looked like she'd waded through a swamp.

She closed her eyes and swayed on her feet. He stopped himself before he reached out to steady her, then berated himself for not doing so. Even if there was some history between them, she was a victim according to Officer Johnson, and he was a cop. She deserved the courtesy he'd give any other person in need of help.

Brad grasped her arm and eased her back toward her chair. "You look exhausted. Sit down before you fall down."

A weak smile pulled at her lips, and she allowed him to guide her back into the chair. "Thank you, Brad. I know this is a shock for you to find me here, but I had to see you."

After she was settled, he pulled a chair up from the other side of the room and sat down facing her. "I didn't even know you were in Memphis. One of the officers said you were found walking on Mud Island last night. What happened?"

Her face crumpled, and big tears rolled down her face. "Oh, Brad, it was awful. I've never been so scared in my life."

No matter how much he'd tried through the years to steel himself when a victim started crying, he'd never been able to ignore a woman's tears. The fact that this was a woman he'd once been engaged to only made it tougher. He swallowed hard and glanced around for the box of tissues he and his partners kept in the office for times like this.

He pulled one out and handed it to her. "Take your time. Just tell me when you feel up to it."

She wiped her eyes and blew her nose. "Let me

start by asking if you saw Grace's interview on the news last night."

He frowned and shook his head. "No. Who did she interview?"

"Me."

"You? What...I mean, I don't understand." He shook his head in dismay. "Whoa, Laura. Back up here. How long have you been back in Memphis? It must have been some time if there's something Grace needs to interview you about."

She glanced down at her hands and twisted her fingers together. "I've been back for over a year now. Grace and I share a house in midtown Memphis. It works for us because she's close to the television station, and I'm near Cornerstone Clinic where I work."

He sagged back in his chair, his mouth gaping open. "A year? And you didn't let me know? What do you do at Cornerstone?"

"I'm a forensic nurse. I counsel patients there, and we contract with the hospital and the police to counsel crime victims. I really enjoy this work."

He stared at her a moment, trying to digest what she'd just told him. "I can't believe I didn't know this. I've seen Grace reporting at several crime scenes in the past year, and she never said a thing about you being back."

Her face flushed. "I asked her not to tell you if she ran into you."

"Why not? I thought she was my friend, too. At least she was all the time we were in school together." A feeling of betrayal flowed over him as the angry words spewed from his mouth.

"Oh, she is, Brad. But I didn't want her put in the

position of having to explain my presence in Memphis to you. After all, we didn't part on the best of terms."

A snort of disgust rumbled in his throat. "That's putting it mildly."

She sighed and straightened in her seat. "Well, no matter what happened in the past, you're a detective in the police department, and I need your help."

Brad took a deep breath and nodded. "You're right. There's no changing what happened in the past. So let's deal with the present. Tell me what happened to you last night."

She looked as if she might say something else, but instead she bit down on her lip and nodded. "I should never have let Grace talk me into doing that interview about my parents' murders."

"What?" He scooted to the edge of his seat, his eyes wide. "Don't tell me you went on television and talked about the car bombing."

"I did. It was totally the wrong thing to do."

A sick feeling started in the pit of his stomach, and he swallowed back the bitter taste flooding his mouth. "That's an understatement. What happened?"

He listened as she related the events of the night before. With each word his heart sank, and he balled his hands into fists at the look of fear in her eyes. She wiped at a tear as she told him how she'd stood in the river with the water nearly to her knees as she'd waited to die, and he clasped his hands together to stop the shaking. He could visualize how she must have looked as she waded from the river and fell on the bank.

"I started walking. I thought I might be able to make it back to the hospital where my car was parked, but the two police officers happened to drive by. They picked me up and brought me downtown."

When she finished, Brad sat silently as he tried to relax and get his heartbeat back to normal. Finally he spoke. "So you never saw the face of your abductors?"

"No."

"When the man spoke to you, was there anything familiar about his voice?"

She shook her head. "No."

"And he told you there would be something on the news about history repeating itself?"

"Yes. It was like a threat that the same thing could happen to me. But I haven't heard the news today. Do you know what it might be?"

He waved his hand in dismissal. "It doesn't matter right now." He let his gaze drift over her again. "Why didn't you tell the officers who picked you up what had happened?"

Her face flushed. "Because I was afraid. I don't want word to get back to these people that I talked with the police. I knew I could trust you to tell me what I should do."

He scowled at her. "I wish you had asked before you did that interview. I would have told you not to do it."

She sighed. "I figured that out for myself when I woke up and found myself tied up and blindfolded. What do you think I should do now?"

He studied her for a moment. "When was the last time you ate?"

She thought for a moment. "Yesterday at lunch. I didn't have time for dinner last night."

He pushed to his feet. "Then the first thing we need

to do is get you fed. I know a place that serves a great breakfast."

She stood up. "But I don't have time for that. I have to go home and get ready for work."

"You're not going to work today. Call in and tell them while I check with my partners about covering a case for me."

She shook her head. "Brad, really I don't have time, and I don't want to take you away from your other cases."

"Laura," he snarled, "don't argue with me. You have just come on the radar of some very dangerous people, and we need to talk about this some more. So whether you like it or not, for the time being we're stuck like glue. Later we'll figure out what we need to do to keep you safe." He pointed a finger at her. "Now call your boss while I get in touch with my partners, then we'll go to breakfast."

He strode from the office and closed the door behind him. He walked a few steps down the hall before he stopped, leaned against the wall and punched in the number of Alex Crowne, his partner.

"Hello."

"Alex, Brad here. I've got a problem at the station, and I need you and Seth to cover for me with the Nathan Carson case at the hospital. Can you do that?"

"Sure. Anything we can help you with at the station?"

He started to tell him about Laura, but Alex still held some resentment toward her. "No, I can handle this. I just think someone needs to be there if Carson regains consciousness. He claimed on the phone to have information about the undercover policeman's death five years ago. If he can talk, see if you can find out what it is. And see if you can get him to tell you who is running Tony Lynch's organization now."

"Will do. I'll check in with you later."

"Yeah, later."

Brad ended the call and turned to go back to his office. He hesitated with his hand on the knob and took a deep breath. Spending the day with Laura wasn't at the top of his list of things he wanted to do, but there wasn't much he could do about it right now.

The murders of her parents might be a cold case, but it was an open secret within law enforcement that Tony Lynch's organization, the same group suspected in Nathan Carson's attempted murder, had been responsible.

The only problem was that there was no evidence to prove it since Tony's henchmen made it a rule to never leave any evidence behind. Which left the question—why did they try to kill Carson and only threaten Laura?

The only way he might figure it out was to stay close to Laura and try to protect her when Tony's men came to finish the job they started last night.

TWO

Fifteen minutes later Laura stared at Brad over the top of her coffee cup and searched his features for any changes since she'd last seen him. She had to admit he was still the most handsome man she'd ever known. His dark unruly hair still tumbled across his forehead, and he pushed it back with his hand every so often, just as he'd always done. His brown eyes didn't sparkle as much as she remembered, but she supposed the things he saw on a daily basis in his job could darken any man's soul.

He stared at her from across the table. "So, you've been back for over a year, and you share a house with Grace Kincaid."

"Yes, Grace has always been my best friend, and we kept in touch after I moved to North Carolina."

Brad nodded. "I know. She used to tell me how you were doing when I would see her. I guess that's why it surprised me that she kept your return to Memphis a secret."

"I explained that."

He exhaled and picked up his cup. "Yeah, you did. Anyway, it's good to see you. I'm sorry it was under these circumstances, though."

"It's good to see you, too. I read in the paper that you and Alex and another detective had been appointed to head up the new Cold Case unit for the police department. I'm glad to see you and Alex doing so well. Of course, I knew from the time I met you during our freshman year in high school you would be successful. The director must have a lot of confidence in you to give you such a promotion."

Brad shrugged. "Maybe, but I really like this new work. It's giving me a chance to bring closure to a lot of families who didn't get answers." He stared at her for a moment. "Grace told me about a year ago that she thought you'd finally made peace with the past and could accept your parents' deaths. What made you do that interview with her and open up all these old wounds?"

Laura wrapped her fingers around her coffee mug and stared at the dark Colombian blend. "I thought I'd moved on, but I guess I haven't. I don't suppose I ever will until the killers are brought to justice. Can you understand that?"

"I can. I hear it every day from other families, but they're not being threatened by people who want to kill them. You made yourself a target when you did that interview."

She nodded. "I didn't think about it at the time, but I did when I was standing in the river." She took a sip of her coffee. "Grace's station had been reporting about your new unit, and she thought it might give the story a personal twist if viewers could hear from a family member wanting a case solved."

He arched an eyebrow. "Well, I can't say I like the twist your story took afterward."

The waitress approached with their breakfast, and they fell silent as she set their plates in front of them. Laura clasped her hands in front of her on the table, bowed her head and closed her eyes. When she opened them, Brad stared at her as if he couldn't believe what he'd just seen.

"What is it?" she asked.

"Since when did you become religious?"

She smiled and put her napkin on her lap. "It's not a question of being religious, Brad. The truth is I turned my life over to God, and I live my life in faith. I'm happier than I've ever been in my life."

"What does your brother think about that?"

"He approves. Especially since he's done the same thing, thanks to the influence of his wife." Brad shrugged and began to spread jam on a piece of toast. "I guess whatever makes you happy is fine. You know I've never had any reason to believe in God. I don't need God or anybody else in my life."

Her forehead wrinkled. "You sound cynical. I hope I'm not the reason for that. I'm sorry for what happened between us six years ago. I've wanted to ask you to forgive me for a long time, but I didn't think I'd ever have the nerve to face you."

His eyes narrowed. "I can understand why. I loved you, Laura, from the first day I saw you at school. We were a couple from then on. I would have done anything to make you happy, and you gave back my ring and walked out on me without a backward glance."

His words were tinged with hurt, and Laura wanted to make him understand what had driven her to do what she did. She set her fork down on her plate and clasped her hands on her lap. "I might have been twenty-three years old when I left Memphis, but I still felt like the ten-year-old girl who'd seen her parents bombed in that car. My brother, Mark, carried the same scars I did, and he wanted me to come live with him in Raleigh. He thought we could help each other. I left for your sake as well as mine."

"That's what you told me, but I wanted to help you, Laura."

Her eyes grew wide. "Oh, I know you did, but I felt like I had to find my own peace. It wasn't fair for me to saddle you with all my baggage. You didn't deserve that. I left here as much for you as for myself."

He grimaced and a grunt of disgust rumbled in his throat. "I'm afraid I didn't see it that way."

She tilted her head to one side and stared at him. "I'm sorry I hurt you, but it was the right decision for us both."

He picked up his fork and scooped up some eggs. "Well, as they say, that's all water under the bridge now. I recovered and moved on." He pointed to her plate. "Let's eat our breakfast. Then we have to figure out what we're going to do about keeping you safe."

Laura stared at Brad for a moment before she poured syrup on her pancakes and began to eat. In the time she and Brad had been talking, she'd sensed a change in him. Instead of the caring man she remembered, he seemed distant and jaded. Had she caused that change in him, or was it his job?

A groan of approval rippled from her throat as she swallowed her first bite of pancake. She hadn't realized how hungry she was. "Thank you for bringing me here and thank you for wanting to help me."

He paused with his fork halfway to his mouth and

set it back on his plate. Then he cleared his throat before he looked up at her. "It's my job, Laura. Don't read something personal in what I'm doing for you. I would do it for anyone needing help. Now eat your breakfast, and then we'll go by your house and get you some clean clothes."

The rebuff felt like a slap in the face, and she struggled not to let her face betray how his words had hurt. After a moment she took a deep breath and nodded. "I understand. I'm sorry I didn't let you know I was back, but I knew you didn't want to talk to me. When I saw the article in the paper that you were heading up the cold case department, I wanted to ask you to look into my parents' case again. Then I decided it was better to let it go, that maybe it wasn't meant for me to know who killed them."

He gave no reaction to her words. "Then why did you agree to that interview?"

"Coming back to Memphis triggered a lot of memories for me, and it makes me angry that the people who killed my parents are still out there somewhere. I thought doing the interview might make somebody who knows something about it step forward. I didn't think that it might also get me killed."

He exhaled and raked his hand through his hair. "It scares me to think how close you came to that happening. But you'd better think about what you really want before you get back on that emotional roller coaster you were on before you ran away."

"I'm afraid of that, too," she whispered.

He leaned forward. "If it means anything to you, one of the first things I did when I went to work in the unit was to pull the files on your parents' deaths and look them over."

Her heart pounded and she sat up straight. "Did you find anything?"

He shook his head. "No. I didn't find anything at the time, but it wouldn't hurt to take another look. Your abduction may give us some leads."

"Like what?"

"We'll question hospital personnel to find out if anybody saw a vehicle leaving the parking lot at the time of your attack. We'll trace the cell phone number of the call you received. Either of those things might lead to something."

"Thank you, Brad."

He shook his head. "You don't have to thank me. It's my job to work on the cold cases we've been handed. But it's not going to be easy for you."

"What do you mean?"

"You've always been a little headstrong, Laura, but listen to me. You don't want me to start something if you're not willing to see it through no matter where it leads."

"I know that."

He shook his head. "No, you think you know that, but cold case investigations can take years. Are you prepared to wait out the time it takes to see this to the end?"

She squared her shoulders and lifted her chin. "I am."

He sighed and nodded. "Okay. Let's finish our breakfast, and we'll go pick up your car at the hospital. Then I think we need to go by your house and let you get cleaned up. I'll take you back to my office. If you'd like, I can pull your parents' file, and we'll look through it."

"I'd like that. Thank you, Brad."

"And another thing. I think you're going to need some protection. I have to figure out how we're going to do that."

She started to protest that she didn't need protection, but the memory of a gun pressed to her back and an evil laugh kept her from speaking. Brad was the trained police officer, and she needed to listen to him. He might not like her very much, but she knew he would do everything possible to protect her.

When she'd agreed to do that interview for Grace, she had no idea that it would lead her into danger. But even more surprising was the fact that her abduction had further fueled the desire she'd tried to suppress for years—to find out who hated her parents enough to kill them.

Now the fire she'd thought extinguished burned in her stomach again, and she wouldn't rest until she had the answers she'd wanted since she was ten years old.

After showing Brad to the den, Laura disappeared into her bedroom, where she'd been for the past forty-five minutes. With three sisters in the house when he was growing up, Brad never had been able to figure out what took women so long to take a shower and get dressed.

With a sigh he leaned back on the sofa and flipped through the television channels. He never had a chance to watch TV in the morning, so he had no idea there were so many talk shows on. He punched the remote again just as his cell phone rang. The number displayed was from the local FBI office.

He muted the volume on the TV and raised the phone to his ear. "Detective Austin."

"Brad? This is Bill Diamond. I just heard about Nathan Carson. How is he?"

Brad eased back into the couch cushions and sighed. "I don't know, Bill. The last I heard they were taking him to surgery. The detectives from homicide were on their way to question his wife, so I left. My two partners should be at the hospital now."

There was silence on the line for a moment until Bill spoke again. "So you're not at the hospital now?"

"No."

"When you head back downtown, why don't you take a detour by here? Let's put our heads together on this case and see if we've missed anything."

"I can't right now. I'm on another case. Is there anything we can discuss over the phone?"

"I think so. Hold on a minute. I want to check on something."

Brad heard a desk drawer open and close, then the rustling of papers. As he waited patiently for Bill to speak again, he thought of the first time he'd met Bill. It was soon after the agent had been assigned to the FBI's Memphis office, and they'd become friends right away. The man's no-nonsense attitude had served him well as he'd risen through the ranks of the agency, and Brad was glad he'd been placed in charge of the office in Memphis.

"Okay, I'm back," Bill said. "I wanted to get out the file I'm keeping on Nathan Carson."

Brad took a deep breath and blew it out.

"The bureau has been watching Carson for a year now. He may have known that and decided to call you because he wanted to get some kind of deal before he was arrested. We believe he holds the key to catching the ring of human traffickers we've been after for years. When you told me he had called you, I thought we might be on our way to shutting down Lynch at last. Now Carson's in the hospital fighting for his life."

Brad nodded. "Somebody had to know he was meeting with me today, but I can't figure out how they could have known. The only people who knew were my partners and you. How could anybody else have found out?"

"Who knows? They might have his phones bugged, or there could be someone planted in his office to keep an eye on him."

Brad's fingers tightened on his cell phone. "Are you sure the case he wanted to talk to me about is connected to your human trafficking ring?'

"It just makes sense that it is. An undercover cop discovers Lynch's organization is dealing in illegal aliens. He's murdered and left on the riverbank. Then we have no leads for five years, even though we've had several unidentified bodies found along the Double Nickel."

Brad frowned. "Double Nickel? Is that some kind of bureau talk?"

Bill's laugh rippled into Brad's ear. "No. We've known for years that smugglers are bringing in illegal aliens on ships down on the Gulf coast. Some of them are sent up the Mississippi River on boats and others are transported on trucks up Interstate 55, which is called the Double Nickel by smugglers of both drugs and humans. The sad thing is, the people who are being brought in paid these people good money to get them into the States. What they don't find out until it's too late is that the men are bound for big farms in the West where they'll be treated like slaves, and the women will end up in brothels."

Brad's stomach roiled. He'd heard these stories from agents for years, and it sickened him that the smugglers always seemed to be one step ahead of the police. Just like with Nathan Carson. Just when they had what looked like a promising lead, someone beat them to Nathan.

"What do you intend to do now?"

Bill sighed. "I talked to the director of the police department. They don't have the manpower to keep a guard posted outside Nathan's room twenty-four hours a day, but we can do that. If Nathan makes it through surgery, we'll have someone guarding him 24-7. I don't want anybody getting to him, and I want to know the minute he regains consciousness."

Brad pushed up from the sofa and raked his hand through his hair. "That sounds good, but I need to tell you something else."

"What?"

"I told you I'm working on another case right now. I think it may be linked to the Carson case, too."

When he'd finished relating the facts in the unsolved case of the Webber murders and of Laura's abduction the night before, Bill gave a low whistle. "The car bombings sound like more than a coincidence. Maybe both cases are tied to Tony Lynch and his organization."

"That's what I think. I'm going to look into the Webber case again and see what I can find out. With any luck we may be able to close two cold case files and catch your human traffickers at the same time."

Bill chuckled. "That sounds like a mighty tall order, but nothing would make me happier. Let's stay in touch."

"Okay. Talk with you later."

Brad ended the call and stared at the phone a moment before he punched in another number. It only rang once before his partner answered. "Detective Crowne speaking."

"Hi, Alex. It's Brad."

"What can I do for you, buddy?"

"I've been on the phone with Bill Diamond and wondered if you'd had any word on Nathan Carson's condition in the past hour."

"No, I'm in the hospital waiting room right now, and he's still in surgery. I suppose the longer he hangs on, the better his chances of survival."

Brad nodded and glanced at his watch. "That surgery sure is taking a long time, but he had a lot of injuries. I'm working on something else right now, so keep me posted."

"No problem. Seth and I will see you later."

"Alex?" Brad blurted out in an attempt to keep him from hanging up.

"Yeah. Is there something else?"

Brad bit down on his lip a minute and hesitated. "Nothing really. I thought I'd let you know Laura is back in town."

There was silence on the other end of the phone for a moment. "She is? Have you seen her?"

"Yeah. That other case I'm working on involves her. I'll tell you all about it when you get to the office."

Alex hesitated before he spoke. "Okay. And how did you react when you saw her?"

"I'm all right. She wants us to reopen her parents' case."

"Well, it's officially an active case. What did you tell her?"

"I told her we would." Brad closed his eyes and rubbed his hand over his face. "Look, we'll discuss this later. I just wanted to let you know we're going to take a closer look at it."

"Sure. I'm up for that."

"See you later."

Brad ended the call and sat back down on the sofa. Maybe he could get Alex or Seth to take over the case. Then he wouldn't have to see Laura. She would probably like that better, too.

It would be more comfortable for them both if they kept their relationship in the past where it belonged. He felt a surge of relief. That's what he'd do—turn Laura over to Alex and Seth. He would tell her he had too many cases right now to devote the time needed for her parents' murders.

On the other hand, he had nothing to fear about being around Laura. Their relationship had been over for six years, and there was no way either one of them wanted to resurrect something that was as dead as their feelings for each other. As a detective with the Cold Case unit, though, he owed her his help. But if he was honest with himself, he owed her for another reason.

He couldn't count the number of hours in the past he'd spent listening to Laura talk about the morning she had watched her parents' car explode right before her eyes. At times her anger and grief had reduced her to hysterics that were only calmed by his holding her in his arms and telling her he'd always be there for her. He'd meant it when he gave that promise, and he wouldn't take it back now.

If Laura wanted to find the answers to her parents' deaths, he would help her. He wanted to be there when they found out the truth.

THREE

Brad didn't speak as he led Laura down the police station's basement hallway. Within this part of the building all the evidence in the department's cold cases sat on shelves, just waiting for someone to find the answers to these unsolved crimes. A feeling of despair washed over Laura at the thought that other families still waited for answers that might never come.

Laura followed quietly behind Brad and stared at his straight back and fists clenched at his side. Did he regret telling her she could look through the evidence in her parents' case? When he had offered, she could hardly believe it. For years she'd wanted to see what the police had discovered during their investigation, and yet she'd feared seeing it, also.

Brad stopped at a closed door and pushed it open. He turned toward her, and a look of concern flashed across his face. "What's the matter? You look like you're having second thoughts."

She swallowed back the uncertainty that washed over her and took a deep breath. It was time to deal with the past. She pushed past him into the room. "I'll be okay."

A long conference table with chairs on either side

stretched nearly the length of the small room, but it was what sat in the center of the table that demanded her attention—a cardboard box with the words WEBBER EVIDENCE written on its side. She pressed her fist to her mouth and groaned.

This was what was left of her parents' lives, a box containing evidence from the scene where they died. Could she really do this? Could she look through the words that investigators had written years ago? To them it had been just another crime scene, and they had probably recorded it in a cold, analytical reporting of the facts. To her, though, it was something more than that.

Maybe she'd been wrong to insist on seeing this. She closed her eyes for a moment and said a silent prayer for strength to follow through on what she had started. She owed it to her parents to get past how uncomfortable she might feel and look at it as a mission to gain punishment for whoever had committed the horrible deed.

"Laura, are you all right?" Brad's voice brought her back to reality.

She took a deep breath and nodded. "I am. Just had a weak moment."

His hand touched her arm. "You don't have to do this."

She turned to him and blinked back the tears in her eyes. "Oh, but I do. If I don't, I'll never be able to look at myself in the mirror again. Thank you for making it possible for me to be here."

"Glad to do it." He glanced down at the floor, moved around her and pulled one of the chairs out from the table. "This box contains all the reports and notes of the investigating detectives. I thought you could look through these first. Sit here, and I'll get all the reports out for you."

She sat down and watched as he began to pull notebooks and files from the box. "You said these are the reports and notes. Does that mean there's more?"

He nodded. "Yes, but those boxes have the physical evidence gathered at the scene. I thought you might want to look at this before you look at those things, like pieces of recovered clothing and surviving parts of the bomb."

She swallowed nausea at the thought of seeing a piece of the polka-dotted dress her mother had been wearing that day. "Thanks, Brad. I don't think I want to see those things right now. Maybe later."

With a sigh she reached out and pulled the first notebook closer and opened it. An hour later other notebooks lay about the table. Brad pulled another one from the box and held it out to her. "Here's the one where lead Detective Matlock kept his notes."

She took it and opened it to the first page. Her eyes grew wide, and she glanced up at Brad. "Well, he didn't waste any time recording who he thought was behind the murders. He's written here that from the beginning he felt that Tony Lynch hired Johnny Sherwood to plant the bomb, but he was never able to link either one of them to the crime."

Brad nodded. "Yeah, he always thought that. Matlock's retired now and lives in North Carolina. I talked to him when I read through this, and he still regrets not being able to pin this crime on Tony."

Laura turned through the pages and scanned the detective's handwriting. Most of the information recapped talks he'd had with individuals thought to be connected to the crime. She stopped when she came to the page of Johnny Sherwood's interview. She read through it quickly and shrugged. "Johnny Sherwood's girlfriend gave him an alibi that he was with her in New Orleans that night. She even produced credit card receipts. One for gas purchased on Johnny's card at a service station just outside New Orleans and another for a restaurant in the French Quarter. Johnny's signature was on both."

"Yeah," Brad snorted. "Detective Matlock never could find out who really used that credit card. Nobody at the gas station or the restaurant could identify who'd signed from a photo lineup. Matlock believed Sylvia had signed Johnny's name on the receipt."

Laura pursed her lips and thought for a moment. "Those receipts appeared at a convenient time for Johnny, didn't they?"

"That's what the police thought. Before they could prove differently, Johnny was murdered in a parking lot of a club owned by Tony Lynch. Vince Stone was convicted of that murder and is serving a life sentence."

"What happened to Johnny's girlfriend?"

Brad shook his head. "I have no idea. I tried to locate her when I reviewed the file, but I came up with nothing."

Laura flipped through the remaining pages of the notebook. "I'd like to read this more carefully, but I don't want to detain you. Do you need to be doing something else right now?"

Brad shook his head. "No, my partners are covering for me today. I'll stay until you're finished. Then I'll get the evidence back to storage."

"Okay."

He scooted his chair closer to hers and reached for the notebook. "I'll follow along as you look through this. Maybe I missed something the first time. Two sets of eyes are better than one anyway."

She smiled up at him. "Thank you for helping me with this, Brad. I really appreciate it."

"No problem," he muttered and directed his attention to the first page.

An hour later they turned to the last page of the notebook. "Well, I guess that's it. Nothing jumped out at me. How about you?"

He shook his head. "No, I didn't…" He reached out and grabbed her hand before she could close the notebook. "Whoa! What do we have here?"

Laura's eyes grew wide as Brad grabbed the edge of a strip of white paper that protruded from a pocket on the inside back cover and pulled it free. "What is it?"

"A photograph." Brad held the picture up, and Laura leaned forward to examine it. They gazed at the image of a young couple standing next to an automobile. The man's arm circled the woman's waist, and her head was tipped back as she gazed at him. Her long blond hair hung down her back.

"I've never seen either one of them before. Who are they?" Laura asked.

Brad turned the picture over and smiled before he held it up for her to read what was written on the back. "'Johnny Sherwood and Sylvia Warner before she married Daniel Hill.' This is the first time I've seen a picture of her, and I had no idea she got married. Every time she's mentioned in the file, her last name is Warner." Brad pulled the photograph back and wrinkled his brow as he studied. "Sylvia," he whispered. "Where are you now?"

"Do you think she might still be in Memphis?"

Brad shrugged. "I couldn't find a trace of her before. But that was six months ago. Maybe I should try again." He pulled his cell phone from his pocket and punched in a number. "Thompson, this is Brad Austin. Do you still have all that information I gave you some time back on a woman named Sylvia Warner? I need you to run that search again, but this time use the name Sylvia Hill. I just found out she got married." He paused a moment as he listened to the person on the other end of the line. "That sounds good. Anything you can find. I'm down in evidence storage, but I'll be back in my office in a few minutes."

When he ended the call, Laura stood up. "Who was that?"

"A guy who's a computer wizard."

"Does he work for the police department?"

Brad smiled. "No. He's freelance, and he helps me out from time to time. He couldn't find anything before. Maybe something will show up with her other name." He looked at the picture of Johnny and Sylvia once more before he put it in his pocket and closed the notebook. "I'll put this evidence back, and then we'll go to my office to wait for his call."

Her uncertainty earlier about looking into her parents' case had disappeared since opening that file. All she could think about was the possibility that Sylvia Warner might still be in Memphis, and she could be the first lead in finding her parents' killer.

A small ray of hope began to take root in her heart, the first she'd felt in nineteen years. At least it was a start, and she didn't intend to give up until this cold case was solved.

Brad glanced at his watch and tried not to sigh. He didn't want Laura to see how impatient he was to hear back from Thompson. The truth was he didn't know how much longer he could sit still. He'd tried to hide his excitement over this first lead by looking over some files, but he really had been staring at the same page for the past fifteen minutes.

Laura fidgeted in the chair across the desk from him and folded her hands in her lap. "What's taking him so long?"

"I'm sure he's doing a very thorough job. You can't rush these things, you know."

She sighed and pushed to her feet. "Don't pay any attention to me. I'm just champing at the bit to find Sylvia."

"Me, too, but it may take…" The ring of his cell phone interrupted his words. He jammed the phone to his ear. "Austin."

"Hey, man, I may have some information for you."

Brad pulled a notepad closer and picked up a pen. "What did you find?"

"Well, the reason I couldn't find Sylvia Warner anywhere is because her name changed when she married Daniel Hill. They were married in New Orleans about two years after she left Memphis. But afterward she dropped off the radar because she started using her middle name, Anne, with her married name."

"So she's going by Anne Hill now?"

"She was, but Daniel died about a year ago. I couldn't find any work records for her during the years she was married, but she got a job a few months ago right here in town. I guess she had to take her old name back because of social security. Anyway, she's living off of Poplar Avenue and working in a barbecue restaurant close to downtown. I'll text you the addresses."

"Great. Thanks a lot, man. I appreciate this."

"No problem. Catch you later."

Brad disconnected the call and within seconds the text arrived with the addresses. He held up the phone. "Looks like we may have located Sylvia. Want to go with me to talk to her?"

Laura jumped up from the chair. "Oh, do I. I can't believe he found her."

He nodded. "That's the way it is when you're working a case. Leads come from the last place you'd expect. This time it was a picture. What do you say we check out the workplace first?"

"Sounds good to me. Let's go."

Minutes later they were on their way to Ribs and More Barbecue near downtown. Brad watched Laura out of the corner of his eye. She hadn't glanced his way since they left the station. In fact she'd been so silent, it was beginning to bother him. He hoped she wasn't dwelling too much on what had happened to her last night.

He tightened his grip on the steering wheel and cleared his throat. "I've been thinking, Laura. Maybe it's not safe for you and Grace to stay at your house for a while."

She swiveled in her seat and stared at him. "Grace won't be there for the next week. She left for London yesterday afternoon right after we taped the interview. She's on an assignment for the television station."

"Well, this concerns me even more. Your abductors had no problem finding where you work. I imagine they know where you live, too. It's too dangerous for you to be there right now. Is there any safe place you can go?"

She thought for a moment. "My aunt and uncle who raised Mark and me live in California now. But maybe Charles and Nora McKenzie wouldn't mind if I stayed with them. Their house is big enough."

"I remember them. They used to come see you and Mark play sports when we were in school. He was working in your father's office when your parents were killed."

"Yes, he interned there when he was in law school and went to work for my father when he graduated. His wife, Nora, was our nanny. She's the one who was with us when the bomb exploded. I don't know what we would have done if it hadn't been for her. She had the police and firefighters there within minutes. They've remained our closest friends since that time."

"I heard Charles is doing well in his law practice. Your dad would be happy for him."

She nodded. "Yes, he would. He said Charles was born to practice law, and he was happy he had a small part in helping him get started in his career. Charles had been working for Dad about two years before the explosion."

"And you think they'd let you stay with them?"

"I know they would. They live in a beautiful house out in East Memphis. In fact, they tried to get me to move in with them when I first came back, but I wanted a place of my own. And of course I wanted to live with Grace. I'll give them a call later."

He glanced at his watch and pointed up ahead. "The restaurant is right up here. Since it's past lunchtime, we can find a table and order a sandwich while we look around."

She smiled. "Memphis barbecue sounds great. It will only get better if Sylvia is working."

As Brad pulled the car into the restaurant parking lot, he looked over the vehicles parked beside the building. It was well past lunchtime, but there appeared to be a crowd inside. His stomach growled at the tangy smell of barbecue sauce drifting through the air when they climbed from the car.

Laura fell into step beside him, and they entered the café. A counter with a cash register on top sat to the left of the door. A young woman with streaks of red in her dark brown hair smiled at them from behind the counter when they entered. "If you'll wait right here, our hostess will be with you in a minute."

At the other side of the room a woman, who Brad suspected was the hostess, stood with her back to them as she waited for a man and woman to take their seats at a table with a red-and-white checkered tablecloth. When they were seated, she handed them both menus and turned. Laura gasped when she caught a glimpse of the woman's face. She might be nearly twenty years older than in the photograph, but there was no mistaking this was Sylvia Warner.

She walked up to them, smiled and picked up two menus from the hostess stand. "Two for lunch?"

"Yes," Brad said.

Her gaze darted from Brad to Laura before she turned. "This way, please."

Brad put his hand in the small of Laura's back and guided her forward as they walked to their table, then suddenly jerked his hand away. His skin warmed at the memory of how he had done that when they were engaged. Did she recognize that he had used the familiar gesture? He hoped not. It had been a force of habit. He needed to be more careful when he was around her. He wouldn't want her getting any wrong ideas.

Sylvia stopped in front of a booth, and Laura slipped into one side without saying anything. He exhaled as he sat down and took the menu from the hostess. Afraid of what he might see in Laura's eyes, he stared down and didn't look at her.

"Your waitress will be with you in a minute." Sylvia turned, and her heels tapped on the floor as she headed back to her station.

Brad opened the menu and began to scan the items. "What are you having?"

Laura glanced up then. Her attention seemed focused on what she was going to order. A wave of relief rippled through him. He saw nothing that suggested she thought his touch had meant anything. She probably remembered what he'd told her when she broke their engagement—that he would never forgive her for how she'd hurt him. He remembered because he'd told himself the same thing every day for the past six years.

Some things in life she might be able to make amends for, but breaking his heart wasn't one of them. That deed was one that could never be undone.

Laura watched as Brad washed down the last bite of his sandwich with a swig of iced tea and wiped his mouth on his napkin. Laura picked up a French fry, nibbled on it and stared at the uneaten half of her sandwich.

He pointed at her plate. "Aren't you going to finish that?"

She leaned against the back of the booth and rubbed her stomach. "I'm miserable. I can't eat another bite."

He glanced around the almost deserted dining room now and leaned across the table. "It looks like most of the customers have left. This should be a good time to talk to Sylvia. Are you ready?"

She nodded. "Yes."

He motioned to their waitress who hurried across the room to their table. She smiled down at Brad and swished her ponytail back and forth. Laura smothered the smile that pulled at her mouth. The young woman had flirted with Brad ever since the meal began, and she wasn't giving up now. She batted her eyelashes at him. "Can I get you anything else?"

"Yes. I'd appreciate it if you'd ask the hostess to come over here."

Her shoulders sagged, and she frowned as she turned to look at Sylvia who was talking with the cashier. "You want to talk to Anne?"

He nodded. "Yes."

"Then I'll tell her." The girl slapped their check down on the table, whirled and hurried across the room to where Sylvia stood.

Laura chuckled and took a sip of her iced tea. "I think you hurt her feelings, Brad."

His eyes grew wide. "Why?"

"I think she wanted you to show some interest in her."

He frowned and shook his head. "You're imagining things."

Laura sighed and picked up her glass again. "Well, I know your glass was kept filled all the time we were eating, and I had to practically beg for a refill."

"Cut it out, Laura," he growled. "We're here on business."

Laura glanced over her shoulder at the young woman huffing toward the hostess stand. She said something to Sylvia who turned and stared at them. A perplexed look covered her face. Frowning, she walked slowly across the dining room until she stopped at their table.

"Carlene said you wanted to talk to me. Was there something wrong with your food or your service?"

Brad shook his head. "No, I just wanted to talk to you for a minute if you have time."

Sylvia glanced from Brad to Laura before she shook her head. "I'm sorry, but I'm very busy. If you have a complaint to make, perhaps you need to talk to the owner."

Brad reached in his pocket and pulled out his detective's shield. "I want to talk to you, Sylvia. Or is it Anne? Which name are you going by now?"

Her eyes widened as she stared at the badge. She swallowed and glanced down at him with fear in her eyes. "I haven't done anything wrong."

Brad shrugged. "I never said you did. I just want to talk to you. Please have a seat next to my friend."

Laura scooted over, and after hesitating, Sylvia dropped down in the booth next to her. "What's this all about?"

Brad reached back in his pocket and pulled out the picture they'd found earlier in the day. He laid it on the table and pushed it across the surface toward Sylvia. "I'm investigating two murders that occurred about nineteen years ago, about the time this picture was taken I'd say. This is you in the picture, isn't it?"

Sylvia picked up the photograph and stared at it for a moment. Tears filled her eyes. "I haven't seen this in years. Where did you get it?"

"It was in the cold case file of the murders of Lawrence and Madeline Webber. Do you remember anything about those murders?"

Sylvia's face paled, and she gasped. "I had nothing to do with those murders and neither did Johnny. He just had the misfortune of hanging out with the wrong people. That's what got him killed."

Brad pushed his plate out of the way and crossed his arms on the table. "I believe you hung out with the same crowd. In fact I think you worked as a singer at the club Tony Lynch owned down on Beale Street." He glanced around the barbecue restaurant. "This is kind of a long way from the gig you used to have down there. What happened?"

Laura could feel the anger radiating from Sylvia's body. She leaned across the table and hissed at Brad. "My boyfriend was killed. Remember? He had nothing to do with those murders. He was with me in New Orleans when they happened. After Vince Stone was railroaded for killing him, I left Memphis. I had no reason to stay."

Brad's eyebrows shot up. "Railroaded? What do you mean by that?"

Sylvia rolled her eyes and curled her lips into a frown. "Vince was as innocent as Johnny. They just happened to be the two that got set up. Johnny for the

Webbers and Vince for Johnny's murder. The police were played real good by some dangerous people."

Laura reached over and grabbed Sylvia's hand. "Lawrence and Madeline Webber were my parents. I was just a child when they were killed. I need to find the people responsible for their deaths. If you know who these people are, please help us."

Sylvia turned to her. Tears sparkled in her eyes. "I can't. They'd kill me, too. I'm sorry about what happened to your parents, but please believe me. Johnny had nothing to do with it."

Brad picked up the picture and slid it back in his pocket. "You and Johnny must have talked about who was involved. Why didn't he come forward and let the police know?"

Sylvia scooted from the booth and jumped to her feet. "Look, mister. I don't know what Johnny thought because he didn't tell me anything. I just know that they're dangerous. Now leave me alone."

Laura reached out toward her. "Sylvia, please. If you have any information that will help us find who killed my parents, tell us."

Sylvia took a step back and shook her head. "You seem like you're a nice lady, but you need to let it go. Don't go looking for answers because you're only going to find trouble."

Brad and Laura both climbed out of the booth. "What kind of trouble, Sylvia?" Laura asked.

Wild fear shone in Sylvia's eyes, and she jerked her head around to glance behind her. "You can't win with these people, Miss Webber. They'll kill you without thinking twice about it, like they did your parents and my Johnny."

Brad shook his head. "If you're afraid, we can protect you."

She held out her hands to keep him from stepping closer and shook her head. "You can't protect me. They're everywhere. They probably already know you've come here today." She cast a nervous glance over her shoulder. "If you want to help me, stay away from me."

Brad reached in his pocket, pulled out his business card and held it out. "Here's my card in case you change your mind about talking to me. It has my cell phone number on it. I'll meet you anywhere you say."

Sylvia stared at the card for a moment before she jerked it from his hand and stuffed it in her pocket. "I'll take it, but don't expect me to call."

Brad nodded. "I understand you're scared, but think about Johnny. You believe he was innocent. Help us prove it if he was."

Tears filled her eyes, and she opened her mouth as if to speak. Then she clamped her lips together, turned and ran through the door that led into the kitchen. Brad raked his hand through his hair and grimaced. "That didn't go too well."

Laura couldn't quit staring at the swinging door where Sylvia had entered. "Do you think we've caused her trouble because we came down here today?"

Brad shrugged. "I don't know. Sometimes doing this job can prove upsetting. I don't want to put anyone at risk for talking to me, but I have to do my job."

"Maybe she'll call."

"I doubt it. She looked like she was too scared. That makes me think she has information that will help solve your parents' case. If I don't hear from her, I'll follow up with her in a few days."

"Will you come back here?"

He nodded. "No, I'll call her and have her come to the station. Sometimes it helps to get information from a subject if the interview is being done on our turf in an interrogation room. Maybe that would make her want to talk."

"And if it doesn't? What will you do then?"

He reached for the check the waitress had left and picked it up. When he straightened, a chill rippled down her spine. The muscle in his jaw twitched, and his cold eyes bore into her. "I don't know what I'll do, Laura. I warned you that sometimes cold cases take years to solve, if they're ever solved at all. Don't expect to look at the evidence one time and find a solution."

"I know that. I didn't mean…"

"When I became a cop, I thought I could help victims of crime, but it doesn't always work that way." He hesitated and took a deep breath. "Then when you left, I believed you would come back, but you didn't. I guess I stopped believing in miracles a long time ago."

Before she could reply, he pushed past her and headed to the cash register. She turned and studied him as he strode across the floor. His words had hit her like he'd shot a handful of arrows at her.

She'd known Brad had been hurt when she broke their engagement, but she hadn't understood the depth of his hurt until now. If he detested being around her, she would have to remove herself from his presence some way. Maybe she needed to leave the police alone about her parents' case for the time being.

Brad and his partners might find something in the

future, but Brad's attitude told her he didn't want her around. Maybe she'd better back off and spend her time concentrating on helping her clients learn to live with their tragedies. She only hoped that one day she could do the same.

FOUR

Neither of them spoke as they got in the car and headed out into traffic. Brad gripped the steering wheel and silently berated himself for the words he'd spoken before leaving the restaurant. He didn't want Laura to get the idea he still had feelings for her after all these years, but he had to admit he hadn't yet arrived at the place where he could forgive her.

He glanced at her out of the corner of his eye. She appeared occupied with staring out the window at the passing scenery, but her clenched hands in her lap sent a different signal. He took a deep breath. "Laura, I'm sorry for what I said back there. I didn't mean to come across as still being angry with you."

She turned her head toward him, and his heart lurched at the tears in her eyes. "This is why I didn't let you know I was back. I didn't want to be reminded all the time about how selfish I was in ending our engagement."

His eyes widened, and he shook his head. "I never said you were selfish."

"No, but you insinuated it. Maybe if you had tried to understand my feelings about my parents' deaths I would have come back."

He bit down on his bottom lip, swerved into the parking lot of a supermarket and pulled the car to a stop. He swiveled in his seat to face her. "Oh, really? That would have been kind of difficult to do since you didn't waste any time in getting engaged again."

Her face turned crimson, and her lips trembled. "How did you know about Chet?"

"How do you think? Grace told me all about it when you got engaged. One of your brother's friends, wasn't he?"

She nodded. "Yes. Mark introduced me to him after I went to Raleigh. He was a DEA agent who worked undercover. He was a good man and a good friend to me. Because of him, I turned my life over to God. And he helped me work through a lot of my feelings about my parents' deaths."

"I thought I did, too. I'd listened to you talk about it every day since we were fourteen years old. Now here it is fifteen years later, and it's still the only thing we have to talk about."

She grabbed the door handle, jerked the door open and jumped out into the parking lot. Anger lined her face as she leaned down and looked at him. "I'm sorry that the most traumatic event in my life caused you some problems. That's exactly why I left. You thought I should just suck it up and go on. Well, I've got news for you, Mr. Austin. I've sucked it up for nineteen years, and it hasn't gotten any better. Now my life appears to be in danger, and I came to you because you're a policeman. You still have no idea what I've been through."

Brad raked his hand through his hair and glanced around the parking lot. Several shoppers had stopped loading groceries in their cars and stared at Laura, whose voice had risen to a high pitch. "Laura," he hissed, "get back in the car. People are starting to watch."

She glanced at a woman who stared at them from a few cars down and then back at him. "There's no need for you to be bothered any longer. I'll call a cab to take me home, and you can go on to whatever else you need to be doing today."

With tears running down her face, she slammed the car door and stormed across the parking lot toward the supermarket's front door. As he watched her go, his heart slammed against his chest, a warning that he'd been way out of line with Laura. Whatever had happened between them in the past had no bearing on his responsibility to her as a victim of a crime.

He had to apologize to her, and he needed to do it now. He yanked the keys from the ignition, jumped out of the car and ran after her.

Laura heard the car door slam, and she looked over her shoulder to see Brad running after her. She increased her pace, but he caught up with her halfway to the building, grabbed her by the arm and whirled her around to face him.

The misery she saw in his eyes made her heart lurch. "I feel like a jerk, Laura. I shouldn't have said what I did. I'm bone tired from not getting any sleep last night, and I haven't recovered from finding you in my office this morning. Please accept my apology. I didn't mean to hurt you in any way."

She shook her head. "No, maybe you were right. I shouldn't have assumed we could pick up a friendship that began so many years ago. I'd hoped that after all this time you'd come to grips with your hatred of me, but it's evident you haven't."

His grip on her arm tightened. "I don't hate you. I never have. I'm sorry if I've given you that impression. Today has been like a dream. I can't believe you're here and that we're back to dealing with your parents' deaths." He glanced back at the car. "Come on. Let's get back in the car. We both need to get some rest. Then we can talk about this rationally."

She jerked her arm free and backed away. "I told you I'm going to call a cab." She jammed her hand in her purse and pulled out her cell phone, but before she could make a call, the ringtone of "Can't Help Falling in Love" filled the air. Without glancing at the phone she pushed the connect button and held the phone to her ear.

"Hello?"

"So you ran to the police."

Her breath caught in her throat at the familiar voice. Her eyes grew wide, and her hand holding the phone trembled. "W-what d-do you want?"

"Last night was a warning. Do I have to make another visit?"

She closed her eyes, and an icy feeling flowed through her veins. It was almost like she was back on the riverbank, and he was telling her to take another step. She summoned up all her courage and took a deep breath. "Leave me alone."

Brad stepped closer to her and frowned. "Who is it, Laura?"

She shook her head and waved him back. "Do you understand me?"

A sinister chuckle drifted to her ear. "I think you're the one who'd better understand. Some things are better left buried. Now why don't you get back in the detective's car and let him drive you home?"

She staggered backward a step as she jerked her head from side to side in a terrified gaze around the parking lot. "Wh-where are you?"

"I'm nearby." He paused, and she thought he'd disconnected. Then his soft whisper sent chills through her. "That red outfit you're wearing looks expensive. I'd hate to see it muddy like your scrubs were last night."

"How did you…?"

A click on the line told her the call had disconnected. She stuffed her phone back in her purse and clamped her hand over her mouth. Brad stepped closer and grabbed her by the arms. "Who was that?"

She tried to speak, but the words wouldn't come. She cast one last terrified glance around the parking lot and took a deep breath. "We've got to get out of here. They're watching us."

Brad's frown deepened. "Who's watching us?"

"The man who abducted me last night. He knew I'd been to the police, and he knew what I was wearing." She clamped her hand over her mouth to stifle her high-pitched voice.

Brad grabbed her arm and steered her back toward the car. "Get in the car, Laura. I need to get you out of here."

She nodded and ran alongside of him as they hurried back to the car. Once inside he cranked the engine and roared from the parking lot. As he sped down the street, he looked in the rearview mirror from time to time. After a few minutes he glanced at her. "I don't think we're being followed. I'm going to take you to your house to get some clothes. You need to stay somewhere else for a while. You mentioned Charles and Nora. Do you think you can go there?"

Laura nodded. "I'm sure I can."

"Good. We'll go by your house so you can get some clothes. Then I'll take you over there."

"I'll need to take my car."

He shook his head. "You don't need to be driving around town alone."

She gritted her teeth and glared at him. "I'm going to take my car. Sometimes I get called out on an emergency at night if a victim's family needs help."

He bit down on his lip and frowned. "You're involved in a tense situation here, Laura. I don't know who these guys are, but we'll do our best to find out. Until we do, I want you to lay low, and let us do our job."

She turned her head and stared out the window without answering him. During the six years she'd spent in Raleigh, she had convinced herself she could live with the unanswered questions about her parents' deaths. She'd even told herself that when she returned to Memphis, but now she knew that was impossible.

The events of last night and today had propelled her past a point of no return, and now she wouldn't give up until she had the answers she'd craved since she was ten years old. Brad wouldn't like her decision, but he couldn't stop her from what she intended to do. The problem was that right now she had no idea how she should proceed.

* * *

An hour later the chilled atmosphere that surrounded Laura and Brad hadn't warmed. He'd waited patiently for her to pack a few clothes, and then he'd followed behind her as they drove to Charles and Nora's house. Laura gave a sigh of relief when they pulled the cars to a stop in front of the elegant Southern colonial house.

Brad was out of his car and reaching into her vehicle's backseat for her bag before she could open her door. She blocked his way as he headed toward the front porch. "What is it?" he asked.

"There's no need for you to go inside, Brad. Nora said when I called that she'd be watching for us. I've taken up enough of your time today. I'm sorry I've been such a problem. I won't bother you anymore. If you make any progress with my parents' case, let me know."

Brad set the suitcase on the ground and raked his hand through his hair. After a moment he took a deep breath and stared at her. "I'm sorry for what I said earlier, Laura. I didn't mean to sound uncaring about the things you've gone through. I was always glad to be there. But this day has been such a surprise. I still can't believe you're back."

"I know. And I realize I should have called you. When I told Grace I was moving back, she told me you were involved with someone. I didn't want to bring up a lot of old memories that might cause you problems."

The muscle in his jaw twitched. "I was involved with someone. In fact I was about to pop the question when she told me she wanted to end the relationship.

She walked away just like you did. It made me wonder what's wrong that I can't make a relationship work."

"There's nothing wrong with you, Brad. Maybe it's the women you choose."

"Yeah, maybe so." He reached down and picked up the suitcase. "But I'm going inside with you. I don't want to leave until I know Nora is here."

"Really, it's not..." Before she could finish the sentence he had climbed the front porch steps, punched the doorbell and stood waiting for her. Laura rolled her eyes as she stepped up beside him. "Okay, I give up."

Before he had time to respond, a young woman wearing a maid's uniform opened the door and smiled at them. She glanced at the suitcase in Brad's hand and then back to Laura. "Hello, Miss Webber. We haven't seen you in a few weeks. I thought you'd forgotten us."

"You know I wouldn't do that, Carla. I've just been busy."

"Well, you're here now, and I'm glad to see you. Come on inside." The maid moved to the side of the door, and they stepped around her into a spacious entry. When she'd closed the door, she looked down at the bag Brad held and reached for it. "May I take that?"

"Carla, this is Detective Austin. He's with the Memphis Police Department. He drove me over here."

A teasing smile pulled at Carla's mouth. "I hope you weren't in trouble, Miss Webber."

Brad held the suitcase out to Carla. "No, she wasn't. Not today at least, but I don't make any promises about the future."

Laura arched her eyebrows and shook her head. "Don't pay any attention to him. We've known each other since high school, and he's always loved to tease me."

A shocked look covered Brad's face. "Who's teasing?"

Carla laughed and glanced from one to the other. "Mrs. McKenzie is on the phone in her office. She said for you to make yourself at home, and she'd meet you in the living room when she's finished. Go on in, and I'll get your things settled in your room. I was told you'd be staying with us for a while."

Laura cast a quick glance in Brad's direction. "I'm not sure how long. Several days anyway."

The woman smiled. "You let me know if you need anything. I told Mrs. Smith you were coming, and she's already baking her famous pecan pie for dinner. She knows it's your favorite."

Laura closed her eyes and inhaled. "I think I can smell it baking. Every time I come here all of you try to spoil me. Maybe I should have moved in here instead of living on my own when I came back to Memphis."

"That would have suited all of us fine. Especially Mr. and Mrs. McKenzie. They tell me you and your brother are family to them."

Laura nodded. "We feel the same about them." Laura blinked back the tears that filled her eyes every time she thought of how Charles and Nora had taken care of them in the days following their parents' deaths. "But don't let me detain you from your work. We'll wait in the living room for Nora."

Carla smiled. "I'll see you later."

Laura waited until Carla had climbed the stairs at the end of the entry before she turned back to Brad. "Thank you for bringing my bag inside, but you don't have to stay. I know you have more important things to do."

He shook his head. "No, not this afternoon. I haven't seen Nora in a while. I'd like to say hello to her." He stuck his hands in his pockets and ambled into the living room with Laura right behind. He stopped in the middle of the room and let his gaze drift across the room that looked like a picture right out of *Southern Living* magazine. "Wow, maybe I should have gone on to law school after college."

Laura crossed her arms and stared at him. "I don't remember you ever wanting to do that. All you talked about was catching the bad guys."

He chuckled and nodded. "Yeah, you're right. I'm more comfortable testifying in the cases I investigate than I ever would have been prosecuting or defending one of them."

She smiled at the memory of how excited he used to get. "I remember how you used to talk about being a policeman. That's all you ever wanted."

A sad look flickered in his eyes as he stared at her. He shook his head. "No, that's not all I wanted. There were other things."

"I know," she whispered. "I'm sorry I hurt you, Brad. I was such an emotional wreck I thought you'd be better off without me."

He took a deep breath. "Well, what's done is done. There's no going back now."

"No, there's not."

He was about to say something else when Nora breezed into the room like a whirlwind. Laura had always thought Nora looked like a walking ad for a jewelry store, and today was no exception. Rings

graced three fingers on each hand, and several neck-
laces hung around her neck. The dangling earrings she
wore bounced up and down when she walked.

"Darling, you're finally here!" Her lilting Southern
drawl made Laura smile. Nora grabbed her in a tight
squeeze before she held her at arm's length and studied her face. "You look like you've lost weight. Have
you been eating?"

Laura nodded. "Yes, I have."

Nora released her and stuck out her hand to Brad.
"Hello, Brad. It's been a while since we've seen you.
How are you doing?"

He shook her hand and smiled. "I'm fine, Nora. It's
good to see you again."

"I read about your new assignment in the paper. Of
course you know which one was the first cold case that
came to my mind. Have you had any leads?"

He shook his head. "No, there's nothing new."

She turned back to Laura, and a frown wrinkled her
brow. "Charles and I saw your interview with Grace
on the six o'clock news last night. He was really concerned about you talking so openly about the murders. In fact he tried to call you several times, but you
didn't answer."

Laura cast a quick glance at Brad. "I had some
counseling sessions at the hospital last night and forgot to check my missed calls."

"We aren't sure if it was a good idea for you to
dredge up all those old memories. You seemed like
you were beginning to accept what happened."

Brad nodded. "My thoughts exactly. Did Laura tell
you what happened after the ten o'clock broadcast?"

"No. What happened?"

Laura took a deep breath and glared at Brad. "I wasn't going to tell Nora. I didn't want to worry her and Charles."

"You have to tell them," Brad said. "You're at their house because it's not safe to stay at yours. They may possibly be in danger, too, because of your actions, and they need to know."

A panicked expression flashed across Nora's face, and she grabbed Laura's arm. "Danger? What is he talking about?"

Laura shrugged and began her story. By the time she'd finished, Nora's eyes were wide, and her mouth had gaped open. She turned to Brad. "What are you doing to catch the people who did this?"

"We don't have much to go on. Laura can't identify the vehicle, and she never got a look at the men. There were no witnesses either at the hospital or on Mud Island. I don't want Laura staying alone. That's why we came here."

Nora grabbed Laura's hands in hers. "You're welcome to stay here as long as you like. We'll watch out for you, and we'll…" She stopped midsentence and put her hand to her mouth. Her eyes grew wide. "Oh, no."

Brad frowned and stepped closer. "What's the matter?"

"I just happened to think. We have a dinner with the law firm partners tonight, and Carla and Mrs. Smith have a Bible study at their church. Nobody is going to be home, but Laura doesn't need to stay alone." She shrugged. "I won't go. I'll stay home with Laura."

"No." Laura grabbed Nora's hands. "I don't want you giving up a night out because of me. I'll be fine."

She shook her head. "No, I'd worry about you here alone."

"I'll stay with Laura."

Laura and Nora both turned to stare at Brad, but Nora spoke first. "I wouldn't want to keep you from any plans you have."

"I don't have anything to do. I'd be glad to stay."

Laura's pulse raced, and she shook her head. "No, really, I'll be okay by myself. Charles and Nora have a state-of-the-art security system that rivals Fort Knox. I'll be perfectly safe."

Nora propped her hands on her hips and frowned. "I don't want to use the same tone I did when you were a child, but I think I'm going to have to." She cleared her throat. "Laura Webber, you are not staying alone. It's too dangerous. Now which will it be? Brad or me?"

Laura looked from one to the other. What should she do? Brad had let her know how he felt about her today, and she felt certain the last thing he wanted to do was spend an evening with her. But he had volunteered to help Nora out.

On the other hand it might give her an opportunity to begin the process of healing her friendship with Brad. He had been her best friend through high school and college, and he would always have a special place in her heart. She wanted to have a place in his heart, too. And she didn't want Nora to miss her dinner.

"Okay," Laura said. "You win. Brad can stay with me."

Nora smiled. "Good. We have to leave by six. Can you be here by that time, Brad?"

"I can."

"Mrs. Smith will leave dinner for the two of you in

the kitchen." She leaned over and kissed Laura on the cheek. "Now I have some things to do upstairs. You stay here and visit with Brad. I'll see you later."

An uncomfortable silence filled the room when Nora left. Laura took a deep breath. "So, I'll see you a little before six?"

He swallowed and his Adam's apple bobbed. "I'll be here."

"Maybe we can use the time together tonight to find a way to rebuild our friendship. I would like that, Brad."

"So would I." He opened his mouth as if to say something else, but he paused and frowned. "I'd better be going. I'll see you later. I'll let myself out."

Before she could protest, he walked past her and out of the room. When the front door closed, she sank down on the couch and covered her face with her hands. She'd never been so exhausted in her life. In the past twenty-four hours she'd relived the horrible memories of her parents' deaths in a television interview, been kidnapped, threatened with death and reunited with a man she had once loved.

She couldn't change the fact that her parents had died in a fiery explosion, but maybe she could do something about the others. The men who'd abducted her had wanted to scare her, and they had. But they'd also done something else. They'd reignited her desire to find the answer to who planted that bomb, and she intended to find the people responsible.

As for Brad, she didn't know if he would ever forgive her or not. She had to try. Seeing him again had reminded her of the good times they'd had together, and she had missed him these past six years. She wanted his friendship again, and she wanted his forgiveness for leaving as she had. That was the first thing she needed to work on, Brad's forgiveness. And she intended to start on that tonight.

FIVE

Brad glanced at the clock on the car's dash as he headed back downtown. Lunch and the trip to get Laura settled had taken up more time than he'd thought. Now it was midafternoon, and he hadn't heard anything from Nathan Carson. He needed to check on him.

Thirty minutes later Brad walked into the critical care waiting room and spotted Nathan's wife and daughter huddled in a corner. They looked as if they hadn't slept all night, but he probably did, too. He ran his hand over the stubble on his jaw and frowned. Maybe he'd have a chance to shower and change clothes before he went back to stay with Laura.

Mrs. Carson glanced up as he approached. A tired smile pulled at her lips as she rose and extended her hand. "Detective Austin, it's good to see you again."

Brad shook the woman's hand and smiled at her daughter. "How is he doing this afternoon?"

Mrs. Carson rubbed her hands across her eyes and sighed. "He made it through surgery, but he's in critical condition. They've let us see him several times, but he hasn't been conscious. The doctors aren't giving us much hope."

"I'm sorry. I know this is very difficult for you. I

don't want to make it harder, but we need information if we're going to catch the people who did this."

She nodded. "I understand. Your partners were here last night, and I told them everything, but I'll be glad to answer any questions you have if you think it will help. I want these people caught as much as you do, and so does Teresa." Tears filled her eyes, and she reached over and clasped her daughter's hand.

Teresa, who appeared to be in her early twenties, squeezed her mother's hand and smiled. "Mom, you know what Pastor John said. We have to put our trust in God no matter what happens. Dad would want us to do that."

Her mother smiled. "Yes, he would." She straightened her back and took a deep breath before she turned back to Brad. "Nathan has been a good husband, and a wonderful father, but he's done some things he regrets. He became so burdened with guilt that he finally sought help from the pastor of the church that Teresa and I attend. He'd fought having a relationship with God for years, but suddenly he did an about-face and turned his life over to God. Now he can't learn enough about God and what He expects from those who believe in Him."

Brad made a mental note of the fact that Nathan Carson had recently experienced a spiritual awakening in his life. That could account for his contacting the police. "Mrs. Carson, has Nathan spoken with you about his calls to me over the past few weeks?"

The woman bit down on her lip and glanced at her daughter. "Teresa, it might be better if you didn't sit in on this conversation."

The girl's eyes widened in surprise. "Why?"

Tears welled in Mrs. Carson's eyes, and she grasped her daughter's hand. "There're things about your father you don't know, and I don't think this is the time to learn of them."

Teresa jutted out her jaw and shook her head. "I've known something was going on, Mother, and neither you nor Dad would tell me. I think the time for secrets vanished when someone tried to kill my father."

Her mother stared at her a moment as if trying to decide what to do. Finally, she bit down on her lip and nodded. "All right." She turned back to Brad. "What do you want to know, Detective Austin?"

Brad pulled a chair over in front of the two women, sat down and leaned forward. "I suppose you know I'm one of the detectives who was recently appointed by the director of the police department to head up a new unit to investigate cold cases."

Mrs. Carson nodded. "Yes."

"Your husband called me a few weeks ago and told me he had information about a cold case that I needed to know about. At first he was afraid to meet with me or even talk to me. He called me from public phones mostly because he was afraid his phones were bugged."

"I know. He told me about it when he first called you. As it turned out, they must have been watching his every move. He worried that he'd done the wrong thing in contacting you."

Brad frowned and rested his elbow on his knee. He leaned closer to stare into the woman's face. "Why?"

She glanced at her daughter before she continued. "Because he was afraid of what would happen to Teresa and me if he told the police what he knew about an unsolved murder case."

Brad scooted to the edge of his seat. "Did he tell you what case it was?"

She nodded. "He said it had to do with the death of an undercover policeman whose body was found beside the Mississippi River five years ago. He said he didn't kill the man, but he knew who ordered the hit. He was afraid they would come after his family if he talked."

A look of horror crossed Teresa's face. "Dad had something to do with the death of a policeman?"

Her mother gripped her hand. "No, he wasn't involved in the murder, but he worked for the organization that killed him. When you were little, he was ambitious and wanted us to have a big house and for you to go to the best private school in town. He became an accountant for an organization that had its hands in all kinds of illegal activities. Drugs, extortion, prostitution, human trafficking—they did it all. He never participated in the day-to-day operation of the group, but he kept track of their money. And it was a lot."

Teresa's mouth gaped open. "My father, the man I've loved and respected all my life, made his money off the misery of other people's lives. How could he do that?"

Tears rolled down Mrs. Carson's cheeks. "He thought he could live with all the things he had to do, but he couldn't."

"Did you know?" Teresa asked.

Her mother shook her head. "I never suspected there was anything illegal going on at his accounting firm. He didn't tell anyone. Then after he turned his life over to God, he knew he had to tell what he knew. His only concern was for us." She looked back at Brad. "He told me about the calls he made to you."

"I assured him the police would protect him and his family if he agreed to testify. And we also were working on getting the three of you in the witness protection program. We were supposed to meet yesterday when he left work, but of course that never happened."

Mrs. Carson dissolved in tears. "Now he's going to die because he tried to do the right thing." A look of terror flashed in her eyes. "Detective Austin, these people are vicious. They'll stop at nothing to keep their secrets. Do you think Teresa and I are in danger?"

Brad glanced from one to the other. "I don't know. I'll ask the department to post a patrol car in front of your house to keep you safe. And the FBI is going to put some guards here at the hospital." He pulled one of his cards from his pocket. "In the meantime, if you have any questions or think of anything you need to tell me, call me. My cell phone number is on there."

Mrs. Carson took the card and smiled. "Thank you, Detective Austin. I feel certain the police will find who did this terrible thing to Nathan. Then maybe he can help you solve the policeman's murder."

"I hope so."

He nodded to the two women and strode from the waiting room. He hadn't told Mrs. Carson and her daughter, but he hoped Nathan could help solve two cold cases. The more he thought about it, the more it made sense. The murder of federal prosecutor Lawrence Webber and his wife had to be connected to his investigation into the illegal dealings of the Tony Lynch crime family. If that was the organization Nathan Carson kept books for, he'd be able to close both cases.

Brad stopped at the elevator and punched the button. As he waited, he thought of his day with Laura and the upcoming evening he dreaded. If Nathan survived, maybe he'd have the answers he needed in a few days. If so, there would be no need to see Laura again. She could go back to her work, and he could get back to his life.

Or should he say his lonely life? He hadn't wanted a relationship with anyone after Laura left, and then he'd met a woman he thought might help him start to live again. She'd done just that until she decided that the life of a police detective's wife wasn't for her. She wanted a husband with a nine-to-five job who would be home for dinner every night, not one who was called into work at all hours whenever a violent crime had been committed.

It had only taken her six months to decide she needed to move on, and she'd dumped him just like Laura had. He'd made up his mind he wasn't about to fall for any woman again. He'd known too many police officers whose marriages hadn't lasted. Since he couldn't even get an engagement to work out, there was no need to think he'd fare any better in a marriage. Better to concentrate on the job and leave love for guys who could make it home to dinner every night.

Experience had taught him he wasn't that guy.

Laura swallowed the last bite of her dessert and moaned with pleasure. "I think Mrs. Smith outdid herself with this pecan pie. It's the best I've ever eaten."

Brad smiled at her from across the table. "I could

tell you liked it. I thought for a minute there you were going to pick up the plate and lick it. But then you always did have a sweet tooth."

Laura laughed and wiped her mouth on her napkin. "Yeah, I did. Do you remember what happened on Valentine's Day when we were freshmen in high school?"

He laughed and laid his napkin beside his plate. "I gave you a box of candy, and you ate the whole thing in one night. You were so sick you couldn't come to school the next day."

"My aunt was so angry with me she wanted to ground me for two weeks, but my uncle wouldn't do it. He said he understood. He couldn't pass up chocolate, either."

Laura rose, reached for Brad's plate and stacked it on top of hers. He smiled up at her. "You could get away with anything as far as your uncle was concerned. I really liked him, and your aunt, too. How are they doing?"

"They're fine. They live in California now. I'm going to meet Mark and his family out there for Christmas. We've already planned it."

He pushed to his feet and reached for the stack of dishes she held. "Sounds like fun."

As he took the plates from her, his fingers brushed hers. A tingle raced up her arm, and her legs trembled. Tonight had seemed like old times with the two of them talking about the past, but she knew there were unresolved issues between them that might not allow them to ever move beyond the hurts from the past.

She jerked her hand away and picked up her coffee cup. "If you'll set those in the sink, I'll wash them later. Let's take our coffee in the den and relax."

He headed toward the kitchen but looked over his shoulder. "I'd better not get too relaxed. You know I was up all night last night. I was afraid I might drop off to sleep during dinner, but thanks to Mrs. Smith's excellent cooking that didn't happen."

She waited beside the dining room table until he had returned and picked up his cup before she led him into the den. They settled on opposite ends of the couch and sipped their coffee for a few moments before Laura spoke.

"Have you heard anything from the man who was injured in the car bomb last night?"

Brad set his cup on the coffee table and nodded. "I went by the hospital this afternoon and talked with his wife and daughter. He's still unconscious. I really hope we get to question him. I believe what he has to tell me will help us solve your parents' murders, too."

Laura settled back in the cushions and took a sip from her cup. "I've been thinking about the family of the man who was injured. Do you think it would help if I talked to them? After all, that's what I do for a living. But with these people, I know what they're going through. I might be able to help them."

"That would be good of you, Laura. I can take you to the hospital when I go tomorrow and introduce you to them."

"Thanks, Brad. I'll see what time I can get away from work to go."

He sat up straight and frowned. "Hold on a minute. Nobody said anything about you going to work. You need to stay home until we're able to get some information from Carson."

"But if he dies, you won't be able to get anything. I can't stay away from work forever. I have bills to pay."

He swiveled on the couch to face her and frowned. "I know you do, Laura, but we need to keep you alive so you can go back to work for good eventually."

She shook her head. "I will be safe once I get to work. If it will make you feel better, I'll get Charles to drop me off on his way downtown."

"Laura, please don't be so…" The ringing of his cell phone interrupted him, and he pulled it from the clip on his belt. He glanced at the caller display and then to her. "Excuse me, this is one of my partners. I need to take it."

He stood, walked across the room and stopped at the double doors that led to the patio before he answered. "Hello."

Laura glanced down at their coffee cups, which sat on the table in front of the sofa, picked them up and headed to the kitchen. While he was talking with his partner, she'd warm up their drinks. The evening that had started so well had disintegrated the past few minutes into a battle of wills over her work. She had to make him understand how important it was for her to be at work. She had patients who didn't need to miss a single counseling session.

She poured the coffee, picked up the cups and turned to go back to the den, but she stopped at the sight of Brad slumped against the kitchen doorjamb. She'd thought he looked tired at dinner, but now he looked like he could barely stand. He opened his mouth, but no words came out.

The cups rattled in her hands, and she set them down on the kitchen table before she approached him.

"Brad, what's the matter? You look like someone just told you the world was coming to an end."

"Oh, Laura," he murmured. "Sometimes I hate this job."

Something was terribly wrong, but she didn't want to push him. Instead she wished she could reach out and wrap her arms around him. That's what she would have done in the old days, but he wouldn't want her to do that now.

She reached out and took his hand in hers. "Tell me what's happened."

He laced his fingers through hers and squeezed until she almost groaned. "That was one of my partners on the phone. He thought I ought to know that a woman's body had been found in a parking lot down on Riverside Drive. She'd been strangled."

Laura shivered. "What a terrible way to die."

"Yes, I think so, too. I find it to be an up close and personal kind of murder."

"If you need to go to the crime scene, go on. I'll be fine until Charles and Nora get back."

He shook his head. "I don't need to go. The homicide detectives will take care of it. They'll bring me up to speed in the morning."

Laura placed her other hand on top of their clenched ones. "Was she involved with one of your cases?"

"Yes. Your parents' case. The dead woman is Sylvia Warner."

It took a moment for the meaning of what he'd said to sink into her mind. Then her knees wobbled, and she felt them give way as she began to fall toward the floor. He jerked his hand free of hers and grabbed both her arms and pulled her back to her feet.

Her breath hitched in her throat as she asked the question she already knew the answer to. "Is she dead because we went to see her, Brad?"

"I don't know," he muttered, "but I would guess that had something to do with it."

Chills raced up her spine, and she began to tremble. Brad put his arm around her shoulders and led her back to the couch in the den. He eased her down and then sat next to her. She reached for his hand again and clasped it in hers as she rocked back and forth in agony.

After a moment her mind cleared, and she remembered the fear in Sylvia's face today at the restaurant. She'd tried to warn them about the people she said were responsible for her boyfriend's death. She probably suspected they'd been followed, and that's why she'd run out of the café so quickly.

A sudden thought hit her, and she turned to Brad. "If Sylvia was right about her boyfriend being innocent of my parents' murders, then she might have been right about Vince Stone being innocent of killing Johnny. Maybe the real killers thought she knew too much and wanted to silence her."

"That's a possibility."

Laura swiveled in her seat and faced Brad. "Where is Vince Stone serving his sentence?"

"At the state prison in Nashville."

"Have you ever questioned him?"

Brad shook his head. "I've never had any reason to. He was found guilty and sentenced to life in prison for the crime he was accused of. But maybe I should. I'll make contact with the warden's office tomorrow and see if I can make an appointment to visit Vince."

"May I go with you?"

"I don't think so. You're not in law enforcement."

"I'm a trained professional who deals with the aftermath of violent crimes every day. I might be able to pick up on something he says that you wouldn't. Please let me go with you, Brad."

He didn't say anything for a moment, and she knew he was debating the pros and cons of taking her along. After a moment he sighed. "Okay, you win. If I take you along, at least I can keep an eye on you."

Laura smiled. "Thank you, Brad, for allowing me to help you with my parents' case. I won't ever forget it."

Her skin warmed from his unflinching gaze. "I may be using bad judgment in taking you along, but I know how important it is for you to find your parents' killers. Just remember I'm the one in charge."

SIX

Two days later Laura hummed along with the music coming from the car radio as she and Brad sped along I-40 on their way to Nashville. Brad looked more rested after getting some sleep. In fact he looked more handsome than she remembered. This morning there was no stubble on his chin, and she found herself glancing at his profile from time to time.

Her gaze drifted down to his long fingers curled around the steering wheel, and she remembered the feeling of them grasping her hand after he'd told her of Sylvia's death. She'd thought of that moment several times in the past two days, and every time it stirred a memory of how close they used to be.

He shifted in his seat as if he felt her gaze, and she looked out the window. "We're about to cross the Tennessee River," he said.

She nodded. "I know. Maybe we'll see some barges on the river today."

He chuckled. "Some things about you haven't changed. I remember I used to spend hours with you down at Tom Lee Park and watch the barges on the Mississippi. I'd have to practically drag you away from there."

She turned to him in surprise. "I thought you enjoyed watching the barges with me."

"I endured it, just like I did all those afternoons with you at the art gallery and the museum when I really wanted to be playing ball with the guys."

His words stunned her, and she sank back against her seat. Had she really been so insensitive to what he wanted? He'd never protested when she told him where she wanted to go. He'd simply nodded and gone with her. The thought that he had loved her enough to do that humbled her, and she suddenly felt very selfish.

"I'm sorry I never knew that, Brad. I guess you have endured more with me than I realized. I must have hurt you over and over when we were growing up, but you never said a word. Why?"

His fingers gripped the steering wheel harder, and his face flushed. "Because I loved you, and I wanted you to be happy."

She blinked back tears and took a deep breath. "I suppose my leaving seemed like my ultimate selfish act to you. You probably felt like I'd been having my own way for years without thought for your feelings and that I walked away without any regard for you at all."

His jaw tensed, but he didn't look at her. "Yeah, something like that."

She reached out and touched his arm, but she could feel the slight recoil and she released him. "I'm so sorry, Brad. I know I sound like a broken record, but all I could think about all those years was the sight of that car exploding. I tried everything to put it out of my mind, but I should have seen that you were there trying to help me." She exhaled and shook her head. "I suppose that's the saddest thing of all. I couldn't care about anyone else's life because I was too wrapped up in my own problems."

"Laura, we don't have to get into this today."

"No, I'm glad to find out how you felt. I hope someday you can forgive me. I'm going to work toward that because I know how forgiveness can free you."

He frowned and glanced at her. "What are you talking about?"

She smiled. "When I accepted Christ, I knew He had forgiven me for all my past sins, but I also knew there were others I'd known who probably hadn't. The Bible tells us to be kind and tenderhearted to each other, and to forgive each other as God has forgiven us. I've prayed ever since that someday you might be able to forgive me. I'm going to continue to pray that prayer because I want you to be free from the hard feelings you have against me. Not for my sake, but for yours. Your life will be so much happier if you can find it in your heart to forgive. I want that for you."

He didn't say anything for a moment. Then he exhaled. "I'm glad you prayed for me, even if I don't pray for myself anymore."

"I suppose that's also a result of my choices. I'll add that to my prayer list, that your faith can be rekindled."

He pursed his lips and stared straight ahead. After a moment Laura snuggled back in the seat and closed her eyes. They didn't speak again until they entered Nashville's city limits.

Brad glanced at Laura from time to time, but she'd fallen asleep. He was glad she had. It gave him some time to think about the things she'd said. Ever since he had walked into his office and found her asleep at a desk, he'd been struggling to keep his distance from her. Unfortunately, it didn't seem to be working. Every way he turned this case seemed to pull them together.

But was he really being honest with himself? Maybe it wasn't the case. It could be that he wanted to be with her. There was no denying that she had put her mark on his heart when they were kids, but he'd told himself for years he had erased her from his mind. Then she shows up back in Memphis, and all he can do is remember the good times. Instead of thinking like that, he needed to concentrate on the bad times—the days, months and years after she walked out on him.

So far he hadn't been successful. Now that she'd told him she prayed for him to forgive her, he was faced with a new decision. Should he forgive her or not?

He shook his head in disgust. Forgiving someone wasn't that simple. You couldn't just say the words. You had to feel it in your heart, and you had to really mean it. He didn't know if he would ever come to that point or not, but he had to admit being with her these past few days had made him question if he had been at fault, too. Before he had time to question himself further, the prison came into sight, and he pulled into the parking area.

Brad turned off the motor and looked over at Laura who was still sleeping. He hadn't had a chance to really look at her since her return to his life, and he sat still drinking in the sight of her. A stray lock of hair hung down the side of her face, and he tucked it behind her ear.

He gasped and drew his hand back like he'd touched a flame. He couldn't believe what was happening to him. He had been sucked in to her problems again, and his protective feelings for her were starting to emerge. He had to be careful it didn't go any further.

He cleared his throat. "Laura, wake up. We're here."

Her eyes fluttered open, and for a moment she appeared confused. Then she pushed up in the seat and checked her makeup in the mirror on the back side of the sun visor. When she'd finished, she flipped it back in place and reached for the door handle. "I'm sorry I went to sleep. I wasn't much company for you on the ride up here."

He shook his head. "It's all right. Are you ready to visit Vince Stone?"

She nodded. "I can hardly wait."

As they walked toward the prison's visitor entrance, Brad let his gaze drift over the buildings scattered across the 132 acres of the site. The new high tech complex was hailed as one of the best maximum security prisons in the country, and he was glad to finally get a chance to see it up close.

Fifteen minutes later they'd been escorted by guards into a room that contained a table with four chairs. They'd barely gotten seated before the door opened, and a man shackled at the hands and feet entered with a guard right behind him. He hesitated at the table and glanced from Brad to Laura.

Brad let his gaze drift over Vince Stone. His graying hair looked like it hadn't been cut in months, and it was tied at the back of his neck. A bushy beard covered most of his face, and his blue eyes darted from him to Laura. But it was his aloof attitude that told Brad he probably wouldn't get information from Vince. Twenty years in prison had turned him into a hardened convict.

But they'd come this far, and he had to try to get Vince to talk with them. He motioned toward the chair. "Have a seat, Vince. We just want to talk with you."

Vince eased down into the chair, and the guard pulled the other chair from the table and sat down behind his prisoner.

Brad clasped his hands in front of him on the table and leaned forward. "Vince, my name is Brad Austin. I'm a detective with the Memphis Police Department and this is Laura Webber. We've driven over from Memphis today to talk to you about a cold case I'm working on."

Vince leaned back in his chair and glared at him. "I don't know nothing about no cold case."

Brad smiled. "Well, I haven't even told you which one it is yet."

Vince shrugged. "Don't make no difference. I don't know nothing."

"I expected you to say that. It's the typical answer from someone who's spent as much time in prison as you have."

A chuckle rumbled in Vince's throat. "You don't know nothing about serving time. Especially when you're innocent of the crime that sent you to prison."

Brad sighed and leaned back in his chair. "Yeah, from what I hear, our prisons are packed with innocent men."

Vince's face turned red, and he gritted his teeth. "I don't know about the others here. I just know I didn't kill Johnny Sherwood."

Brad leaned forward again and stared at Vince. "Maybe you didn't. I have to admit I've had my doubts over the past few days."

"Yeah, I'll bet. You just want something from me."

"I'm trying to find a killer, and in finding him it might prove whether or not you were telling the truth."

Vince frowned. "I don't understand. Whose killer?"

"Lawrence and Madeline Webber's killers. Do you remember when that happened?"

Vince's eyes grew wide, and he tried to push up out of his chair. His feet slipped, and he fell back down. "I didn't have nothing to do with that bomb."

"I didn't say you did, but it was still what ended you up here. There are some people who believe Tony Lynch set Johnny Sherwood up for the murders, then turned around and set you up for Johnny's murder. It all worked out well for Tony. The Webbers were dead, Johnny was thought to be the murderer and you went to prison for life."

"Do you think that?" Vince snarled.

"I don't know what to think. You tell me, Vince."

Vince's shoulders relaxed, and he closed his eyes a moment. "I won't lie and tell you I had nothing to do with Tony Lynch. I was on his payroll. I peddled drugs for him, transported prostitutes to other cities for him and I put the muscle on businesses that weren't paying for their protection. But I never murdered anybody."

"Then how did Johnny die?"

"I don't know. All I remember is that one of Tony's guys came up to me in the club he owned down on Beale Street and told me to bring in a briefcase out of Tony's car in the back parking lot. I walked out the back door, and the next thing I know I'm waking up to the cops telling me I'm under arrest for killing Johnny. His body was right next to me in the parking lot. The cops thought Johnny must have gotten in one good lick and knocked me out before he died."

"Who was the guy who told you to go to the parking lot?"

"It was some college-type guy who worked for Tony. Everybody said he was grooming him to take over his business when he retired."

Brad's heart skipped a beat at the mention of Tony's successor. "What was his name?'

"It was…" Vince suddenly stopped talking, leaned back in his chair and smiled. "I see that got your attention. You must want the name of the guy who now controls the largest crime family in the South mighty bad."

"Yes, the police want his name."

"Well, if you want me to give up what I know, you're gonna have to do something for me."

"Like what?"

"Get me out of here. I want to go home to my wife."

Brad shook his head. "I can't get you out."

"The D.A. can. Tell him I know lots of things he'd find interesting about Tony Lynch's family, and I'll testify in court. But he's got to pay for it. Get me out of here and send my wife and me into witness protection, and he'll have so many convictions he won't have to worry about getting elected again. He can retire in office."

"I don't think he'll…"

"He will if he wants to get rid of the Lynch family." Vince glanced over his shoulder at the guard. "Now I want to go back to my cell."

The guard rose and helped Vince to his feet. Laura jumped to her feet and clenched her fists as he turned and shuffled to the door. She cast an anguished look at Brad. "Do something. Don't let him leave like this."

Brad pushed to his feet and shook his head. "I'm sorry, Laura. There's nothing more I can do right now."

The guard opened the door, and Vince took a step to leave. "Wait!" Laura rushed over to Vince.

She tried to push past the guard, but he blocked her way. "Stay back, ma'am."

"Please, Mr. Stone." Tears filled her eyes. "Lawrence and Madeline Webber were my parents. My brother and I were only children when they were killed. If you know anything about their murders, please help us."

Vince turned his head and stared at Laura over his shoulder. For a moment Brad thought her impassioned plea might weaken his resolve to remain silent, but then he straightened his shoulders and shook his head. "I'm sorry for your loss, ma'am, but I've lost a lot, too. My wife had a miscarriage after I was arrested, and she's spent the past twenty years visiting me in prison. We won't never have any kids, but maybe we could spend the last of our years together." He glanced at Brad. "Talk to the D.A. and get back to me."

Laura watched as Vince hobbled down the hallway headed back to his cell. When she finally turned around, she walked over and stopped in front of Brad. "That man may hold the key to who killed my parents. Why didn't you try to make him tell you?"

Brad raked his hand through his hair and shook his head. "I talk to guys like Vince all the time. He's not interested in helping you unless he can get something in return. Our best bet is for me to take what he's said to the D.A. Maybe a deal can be worked out. That's how a lot of our cases are solved."

"Do you think the district attorney will be interested in what Vince has to say?"

He nodded. "I think there's a good possibility. I don't know about getting him out of here, but he might get him transferred closer to home in a minimum security prison. I'll push for the witness protection program, but that may be out of the question. Vince has done some bad things in his past. But in his favor is the fact that he's spent the past twenty years in prison. It's just my gut feeling, but I believe he's innocent of Johnny Sherwood's murder."

"I do, too."

Brad placed his finger under her chin, lifted her face and stared into her eyes. "I'm not giving up just because Vince wouldn't cooperate today. I'll keep working, and we'll eventually solve your parents' murders."

She smiled, and his heart lurched. "Thank you, Brad. I knew you would help me."

He swallowed hard and let his hand drift back to his side. "There's nothing more we can do here today. How about if we grab some lunch at the restaurant where I eat every time I come to Nashville?"

She smiled. "Some Italian place, I suppose."

He grinned. "You know me well."

"Yes, I guess I do." Her gaze drifted over his face, and his skin warmed from the contact.

He watched as she left the room, and suddenly he was glad she was with him today. Maybe Vince's words about what he and his wife had lost reminded him of what he and Laura lost when she left. Since then, there had been too many lonely lunches and dinners, but today there wasn't.

Laura was back, and he wanted to enjoy whatever time he had with her.

The sun had begun to set when Brad pulled the car to a stop in front of Charles and Nora's house. Laura glanced at the clock on the car's dash. "I've probably missed dinner, but I'm still stuffed from lunch. I liked your restaurant choice."

Brad turned off the engine and settled back in the seat. "I'm glad you did. Maybe we can try it again somctime."

Laura swiveled and faced him. "Do you think you'll be going back to Nashville?"

"I don't know. It all depends on the D.A. If he's interested in pursuing Vince as a witness, he'll probably want to send one of his own people. Of course, I'm sure they'll keep me informed of what's going on."

"I'm sure they will." She paused for a moment before she broached what was really on her mind. "Brad, I need to talk to you about something."

"What?"

"I know you've said you want me to lay low for a while, but I really need to go to work tomorrow."

"We've been through this before. I don't think…"

She held up her hand to stop him. "I know you're only trying to protect me, but I've been off for three days now. I have some counseling sessions I need to attend tomorrow. The clients are just beginning to make some progress, and I don't want anything to interfere with that. I'll be at Cornerstone Clinic all day. I won't go out of the building."

"But how will you get there?"

"I'll drive my car. Charles said he'll follow me and see me inside, and he'll come by tomorrow afternoon. I'll be safe, and you won't be bothered with me."

A sad look flickered in his eyes. "You haven't been a bother to me. I enjoyed having you with me today."

"And I enjoyed it, too. But you can't put your job and your life on hold to play nursemaid to me. I'll call you if I see anything suspicious."

He hesitated before he answered. "If that's what you want, I guess I can't change your mind. But tell Charles there won't be any need for him to come by tomorrow afternoon. I'll pick you up, and you can go to the hospital with me so you can meet the Carsons. Then we can grab a bite of dinner before you come home."

Her heart fluttered, but she tried to keep from letting him know how much the invitation thrilled her. It wasn't exactly a date, but still he'd said they would go to dinner. "All right." She glanced back at the house. "Would you like to come in and say hello to Charles and Nora?"

"Yeah, I would."

He hopped out of the car, hurried around to the passenger door and opened it for her. When they entered the house, she led him to the den where Charles sat at a desk in the corner of the room, with what looked to be a stack of legal papers in front of him. Nora was settled on the sofa reading a book.

Her heart warmed at the sight of the two who had always been there for her and her brother. Nora looked up when they walked in the door and sprang to her feet. "It's about time you two were getting home. I've been out of my mind with worry."

Charles got up, pulled off his reading glasses and laid them on the desk. He rubbed his eyes and chuckled. "Nora is exaggerating a bit, Laura. She knew better than to worry about you when you're with Brad." He strode across the floor and stuck out his hand to Brad. "How did the trip go?"

Brad shook Charles's hand and frowned. "Not too well, I'm afraid. Vince Stone still denies he had anything to do with murdering Johnny Sherwood."

"I would expect him to say that," Charles said. "He denied it all through his murder trial."

Laura turned a surprised look at him. "Did you go to his trial?"

He frowned, and his dark eyes flashed. "I attended every day of it. I hoped something would be revealed that would lead us to who killed Lawrence and Madeline, but nothing ever did."

"We may have had a lead today. Vince claimed to know the identity of the person Tony had picked to take over as head of his organization." After she'd spoken, Laura wondered if what Vince had said would be considered privileged information. She glanced at Brad. "Is it all right to tell Charles and Nora?"

Brad chuckled. "It's too late to ask permission after you've already done something."

Charles turned a questioning look to Brad. "Do you think that might help us find the killers?"

Brad shrugged. "It might. Vince claims he was told to go to the parking lot by the man Tony Lynch had picked to be his successor. He says once he got there he was knocked out and framed for Johnny's murder. Even if we can't find the killers, with the name of

Tony's successor we could put a stop to their activities now."

Charles's eyes grew wide. "This sounds like it could be the break we've been waiting for. What is the name, or is it information you can't share?"

"I wouldn't be able to share it if I knew it, but he hasn't told us yet. I have a feeling it's not going to be long before he does."

The anger that Laura had often seen on Charles's face through the years returned, and he gritted his teeth. "It's about time he told what he knows. We've always believed he had information that could help solve this crime. Somebody has to be brought to justice for what they did to Lawrence and Madeline. There's not a day that goes by that I don't think of that terrible morning."

Laura heard the emotion in his voice, and she looped her arms through his. He looked down at her hand and patted it. "Charles," she said, "you worked with Dad on the case against Tony Lynch. Do you remember his saying anything, or seeing any mention of a young college-type who might have worked for Tony?"

Charles pursed his lips and thought for a moment. Then he slowly shook his head. "Not that I can remember." Then his eyes grew wide, and he nodded. "But come to think about it, there was a young guy who was in the courtroom every day during Vince's trial. Once during a break I saw him in the hall talking to several men who were known to work for Tony Lynch."

"Do you remember his name?" Brad asked.

"Yes, because I know him now as a fellow member of the Tennessee bar. His name is Lucas Pennington.

He has a big law firm in one of the old buildings down on Front Street."

Brad frowned. "Lucas Pennington? I've heard of him. He donates to every charity in town."

Charles laughed. "Yeah. I've often wondered why."

"Maybe I'll have to find out." Brad glanced at his watch. "But not tonight. I need to be going." He glanced at Laura. "I'll pick you up at work tomorrow afternoon."

Laura turned to Nora. "I'll see Brad out, then I think I'll go on up to bed. I'm tired. I need to be up early in the morning to get to work."

Nora kissed her on the cheek. "Good night, darling. We'll see you at breakfast."

Laura led the way to the front door, and Brad followed. When she opened the door for him, he stepped out onto the porch, turned and smiled at her. "Thanks again for going with me today. I had a good time."

"I did, too, Brad. I'll see you tomorrow afternoon."

She watched him go down the steps and drive away from the house before she closed the door and leaned against it. The day really had gone rather well. She and Brad had gotten along better than she expected, and they possibly had picked up information that would help find her parents' killers.

Now all she could do was pray that they would soon have the answers she'd wanted for all these years. And maybe in the process she and Brad could heal their battered friendship.

The fact that he wanted to take her to dinner tomorrow night sounded promising. Perhaps they'd already begun the healing process. She hoped so.

SEVEN

Brad took a sip of coffee from the cup he'd poured in the department's break room as he sauntered down the hall toward his office. For some reason he felt better today than he had in weeks. He'd slept well last night, and he couldn't wait to get to work this morning.

The first thing he planned to do was call the district attorney's office and set up an appointment. The possibility that he'd found a link to the Webbers' case had him pumped this morning, or at least he thought that was what had him feeling like he could conquer the world.

He'd almost reached his office when Alex Crowne, his partner and friend since high school, caught up with him. "I thought you were supposed to be in court this morning to testify in that last case you closed right before we got our new assignment."

Brad shook his head. "Not for a couple of hours yet. I needed to come into the office to make a phone call about my trip yesterday."

"How did that go?"

"It went well. In fact I hope it's going to lead to a break in the Webber case."

By the time Brad had finished relating the events

of the day before, he and Alex had arrived at their office. When they walked into the large room with the three cubicles, Seth Dawtry, the third cold case detective, rose from behind his chair and sat down on the edge of his desk. "Finally decided to show up, huh? I thought I was going to have to come looking for you."

Brad laughed and glanced at Alex. "Correct me if I'm wrong, but I believe Dawtry is the one who likes to oversleep in the mornings."

Alex nodded. "You sure got that right. Seems like we had to call his apartment last week to see if he was coming to work."

Seth's cheeks turned red. "Aw, come on, guys. You know I was taking that cold medicine and couldn't get awake."

Alex elbowed Brad in the ribs and grinned. "Yeah, cold medicine. A likely excuse I'd say."

"Me, too. I think that what really happened was…" Before Brad could finish his sentence, the phone on his desk rang. He hurried across the room and picked up the receiver. "Detective Austin, Cold Case unit."

"Detective Austin, this is Chief Davis."

Brad arched his eyebrows and turned to face Alex and Seth who'd stepped closer. Alex mouthed the words *the chief,* and Brad nodded. "Yes, sir. How can I help you this morning?"

"I believe you went to Nashville yesterday and visited with Vince Stone at the prison."

"Yes, sir. I was going to come to your office in a few minutes and brief you on the meeting."

Chief Davis exhaled, and the rippling breath held the sound of a death knell. "I'm afraid I have some bad news for you, Detective."

Brad tightened his grip on the telephone receiver. "What is it, sir?"

"I just had a call from the deputy warden's office at the prison. Vince Stone died this morning."

"What?" Brad realized the word had come out in a shout, but he couldn't help it. He sank down in his desk chair, closed his eyes and shook his head. "H-how did it happen?"

"From what I gathered, Vince was a bit vocal last night on the cell block about how he had some information that was going to blow a cold case wide-open, and it was going to give him a free ride to a new life. This morning, he was stabbed to death in the shower."

"No, no, this can't be happening," Brad groaned.

"I'm afraid it is. Did Stone tell you anything yesterday that could help you solve the case?"

"No, sir. He said he had some information he wanted to sell in exchange for a get-out-of-jail-free card. I was going to talk to you about taking his request to the D.A. I don't guess there'll be any use in doing that now."

"I guess not." The chief was quiet for a few moments. "Don't let it bother you too much, Austin. You've been on the force long enough to understand if there's one lead, there has to be another one somewhere else. Just keep looking. You'll find it."

"Yes, sir. I will. Thank you for letting me know."

Alex and Seth were beside him before he could get the phone hung up. "What happened?" Alex asked.

"Vince Stone was killed this morning."

"How?" Alex and Seth spoke at the same time.

"He was stabbed to death in the shower. The chief said he talked a lot last night about having some information that was going to blow a case wide-open."

Alex rubbed his chin and shook his head. "We always thought the Lynch organization was spread out across the South. No surprise it reaches into prison, too." He put his hand on Brad's shoulder and squeezed. "I'm sorry about this. It's the best lead we've had on this case since it happened."

Brad nodded. "Yeah, I sure hate telling Laura about this."

Seth glanced from Brad to Alex. "You guys have to remember I'm not from Memphis. I don't know all the background on that case like you do."

Brad sighed. "Yeah, sorry about that."

Seth listened as Brad told him about the case that had gone unsolved for nearly twenty years. When he finished, Seth nodded. "And the daughter, Laura, is the one you were engaged to at one time?"

"Yeah, she and her brother lived with their uncle and aunt. When Laura was a freshman in high school, they decided to pull her out of public school and put her in the private school that Alex and I attended. That's when I met her. We dated all through high school and college. We were planning our wedding when she broke the engagement and moved to North Carolina to live with her brother."

"But she's back now?"

"She's back." Brad sighed. "And she's determined to find out who killed her parents. She's going to be really upset about Vince's death."

"Are you going to call her and tell her?" Alex asked.

"No, I'll tell her this afternoon. I'm going to pick her up and take her to visit the Carson family at the hospital. I thought she might be able to help them."

Alex frowned and shook his head. "Be careful. I remember what you were like when Laura left. I'd hate to see you put through all that again."

"You don't have to worry about me. That's all yesterday's news. I've buried any feelings I had for Laura." He glanced at his watch. "I'd better be heading to court. They might get to my case earlier than expected."

He started toward the door, but Alex called after him. "Wait."

Brad stopped and turned around. "What?"

Alex stared at him a moment before he shook his head. "I was going to warn you about Laura again, but I guess you can take care of yourself."

"I can, Alex, but I appreciate the thought. Don't worry about me. Laura and I were over a long time ago."

Before Alex or Seth could say anything else, he turned and hurried out the door. As he walked toward the elevator, he wondered who he was trying to convince. Was it Alex, or was he trying to make himself believe it?

He stopped at the elevator and thought about how much he'd enjoyed being with her yesterday. Also the first thing he'd thought about this morning when he woke up was that they were going to dinner tonight.

He punched the down button harder than he'd meant to and shook his head. He had to stop thinking like this. The relationship he and Laura had was over long ago, and there was no going back. There was no way he was going to give Laura the opportunity to rip his heart out again.

Laura parked her car in the back parking lot at Cornerstone Clinic and waved to Charles, who waited in his car for her to enter the building. She'd tried to sound confident last night when she'd talked to Brad about coming to work today, but she'd really had some misgivings.

All the way to the clinic she'd glanced in the rear-view mirror from time to time just to make sure that Charles was still following her. Only once did a car get between the two of them, but Charles had managed to get around the vehicle and behind her again without any trouble.

He watched until she'd opened the clinic's door before he waved and drove back into the morning traffic. Laura took a deep breath and headed down the hallway to her office. She dreaded all the work that had probably piled up on her desk since she'd been out. In a way, though, it was a blessing. She needed something to keep her busy so she didn't think about everything that had happened in the past few days.

She was about to step into her office when Josh Nelson, an RN at Cornerstone, emerged from the break room. A smile lit his face when he saw her. "Hey, Laura. We've missed you the past few days. Dr. Jones said you were under the weather. I hope you're feeling better."

"I'm fine, but I may not be after I see all the paperwork that's been left on my desk since I've been out."

Josh laughed and followed her to the door of her office. He leaned against the side and sipped his coffee as he watched her settle behind her desk. "I really am glad to have you back."

Laura sat down in her chair, opened the bottom desk drawer and stuck her purse inside before she answered. "I'm glad to be back, too." She pointed to the stack of papers on her desk and sighed. "This is why I don't like to miss work. It takes forever to get caught up when I get back."

Josh ambled into her office, dropped down in the chair facing her desk and stretched out his legs in front of him. "A lot of my time is spent now on record keeping, but we have to do it in our profession."

Laura exhaled and picked up the report on the top of the stack. "I guess I might as well dig in. I have counseling sessions scheduled off and on all day. If I don't get to work, I may be here later than I would like."

"I'd be glad to help you out with some of that today during my downtime. In fact, if you want to save it until after work, I'd be glad to help you then. I could go to that burger place down the street and get us something to eat. Then we could eat while we're getting you caught up."

Laura hesitated. Ever since he'd started at the clinic, Josh had tried to get her to go out with him. She'd put him off time after time, but he always asked again. She had to admit he was a good-looking guy and fun to talk to, but she'd never been able to accept his invitations. Several of the other unmarried nurses at the clinic had told her she was crazy to pass up an opportunity to go out with the eligible bachelor, but somehow she didn't feel an attraction to the handsome young RN.

Laura leaned back in her chair and smiled. "Thanks for the offer, Josh, but I have plans for tonight."

His eyebrows arched, and he straightened in his seat. "Do you have a date?"

She'd been asking herself that same question ever since Brad had suggested they go to dinner, but there was only one possible answer. Brad really wanted to help the Carsons, and he thought she might be able to give them some comfort because she'd experienced what they were going through. Dinner was his way of thanking her for helping him.

"No, it's not a date. A friend and I are visiting a family at the hospital, and we're going to get something to eat afterward."

He smiled and leaned back in his chair. "I didn't think you'd been seeing anybody."

She shook her head. "No, I'm still adjusting to being back home. I haven't had time to develop any relationships."

"That's good news. You know I've tried to get you to go out with me ever since I started here, but you always have an excuse. I keep thinking I'll break you down, and you'll go just because you feel sorry for me. Maybe I'm fooling myself. If I am, it's time you leveled with me. Am I wasting my time?"

Laura swallowed hard and glanced down at her fingers that had curled around the report on her desk. She liked Josh a lot, and he was one of the most competent nurses she'd ever worked with. But the chemistry between them wasn't there. She didn't feel as at ease with him as she did when she was with Brad.

She flinched at the thought that had just flashed into her mind. Had she allowed herself to become too relaxed with Brad in the past few days? If so, she needed to be careful. She and Brad might become friends again, but she didn't think he would ever trust her enough to give her a second chance.

Josh cleared his throat, and she realized he was waiting for an answer. "I'm sorry, Josh. I like you a lot, but I don't think we could ever be anything but friends. There are a lot of women who work around here who would love to go out with you. Why don't you give some of them a try?"

He stared at her for a moment, a sad smile pulling at his lips, before he exhaled and stood. "Maybe I will." He pushed up out of his chair and glanced at his watch. "For now, though, I'd better get ready for Dr. Jones's first patient. I'll see you later."

Laura watched him go, but she couldn't think of anything else to say. She and Josh had worked together well, and she hoped their conversation wouldn't cause a problem in their professional relationship.

With a sigh she picked up the top report on the pile and began to read it. After a few minutes she laid it aside and leaned back in her chair. It was no use. She couldn't concentrate. Her talk with Josh had made her focus on what she should have thought about six years ago.

Through the years she'd often asked herself if she'd done the right thing when she left Memphis, and she'd come to the conclusion that she had. She needed to get away from familiar places that reminded her of a traumatic time in her life, and being in Raleigh with her brother had given her a lot of comfort.

The one thing she regretted was the way she had left Brad. In retrospect, maybe she should never have broken her engagement, but only gone to stay with her brother for a short period. But she and Brad had argued, and then she wouldn't back down.

Once she'd gotten to Raleigh, she'd started a new life, met Chet and convinced herself she loved him. But in her heart she'd always known the truth. No other man would ever understand her like Brad did, and she'd given him her heart a long time ago. Seeing him again had convinced her that it still belonged to him.

The sad thing was that she had hurt him so badly he would never want her back. Now she had to learn to live with that thought.

Tears filled her eyes. She couldn't let anyone she worked with see her cry. She jumped up from her chair, hurried to close the door, then leaned against it. Suddenly she wanted to hear Brad's voice, and she ran back to her desk. He would probably think she was crazy to be calling him so early in the morning. He might even see her name on caller ID and ignore it, but he didn't. He answered on the first ring.

"Good morning, Laura."

Her breath hitched in her throat. What did she want to say? Why had she called? "H-hello, Brad. Are you at work yet?"

"I'm on my way to court. I just parked in the garage by the courthouse and am walking to the elevator. I'm testifying in an old case today. Did you make it to work all right?"

"I did. Charles followed me all the way, and I'm safe inside my office."

"I'm glad. Did you want something?"

"Uh, no, I…I just thought I'd check in with you. Let you know I got to work."

"I'm glad you did." He hesitated a moment, then said something she couldn't understand.

"What did you say?"

"There were some people waiting to get on the elevator. I told them to go on, I'd take the next one. I was afraid I would lose your call in the elevator."

Suddenly she felt embarrassed. She had nothing to

say to him and had no reason to be calling. He must
think she'd lost her mind. "I don't want to keep you.
Go on to court, and I'll talk to you later."

"No, don't hang up." A sense of urgency sounded
in his voice.

"What is it?"

"I was wondering…do you have any plans for
lunch? I could bring some sandwiches to the clinic,
and we could find a place outside, somewhere to eat.
Maybe go over to Overton Park like we used to." He
paused. "That is if you want to."

Her heart pounded in her chest. "I would like that
very much. Call me when you get here and I'll meet
you in the back parking lot."

"I'll do it. See you later."

"Bye, Brad."

She disconnected the call and sat there smiling for
a few minutes. Maybe Brad had started to think they
might be able to save something from their relationship, too. The thought made her feel better than she
had in days. She laid the phone down and picked up
the first report just as the phone rang. Brad again?

Without looking at the caller ID, she raised the
phone to her ear. "Hello?"

"So you're back at work."

Her eyes grew wide at the sound of the familiar
voice. Her body grew cold as if the water of the Mississippi River was still lapping at her legs. "Wh-why
are you calling me?"

"I just wanted to know if you're feeling better after
your dip in the river."

"Leave me alone. Quit calling me."

A sinister chuckle echoed in her ear. "Aw, don't

be that way, Miss Webber. You should be feeling really good after your visit at the prison yesterday. That Vince must have gotten your hopes up real high. Too bad he had to brag about it last night."

Her hand trembled, and she gripped the phone tighter. "What are you talking about?"

"It just don't pay to brag in prison about what you're gonna tell the cops. It'll get you killed every time."

"Killed?" Laura sprang to her feet and grabbed the desk with her free hand to steady herself. "Did someone kill Vince?"

The man sniffed. "I'm afraid so. Poor old Vince. He never saw it coming. I thought maybe your boyfriend had already told you. I'm sorry to be the bearer of bad news."

"You are a despicable person!" she screamed. "How can anyone talk about taking someone's life in such a callous way?"

"Yeah, it's too bad he's dead. Now we'll never know what he could have told the D.A., will we?"

Laura's body shook, and she felt dizzy. "Let me tell you something, mister. You may think you're safe, but you're not. I intend to find out who you are and what you had to do with my parents' deaths. Then you can see what it's like in prison."

A loud laugh rumbled over the phone. "Dream on, lady. You won't ever find out the truth. Oh, and by the way, I really like that yellow dress you're wearing today. It looks so much better than those scrubs."

Before she could answer, the call disconnected. She looked down at the yellow dress she'd chosen this morning, and the truth hit her. If he knew what she was wearing, he had seen her. Fear rolled through her body, and she sank into her chair.

She'd had nightmares for twenty years about her parents' deaths, but suddenly things had changed. New nightmares now stalked her in the cold light of day. Maybe it would have been better to stay in Raleigh, but it was too late now. She was back in Memphis, and she had to face whatever awaited her.

EIGHT

Brad pulled the car to a stop in the parking lot at the back of Cornerstone Clinic, reached for his cell phone and punched in Laura's number. It only rang once before she answered.

"Hello?"

"Hi, Laura. It's Brad. I'm in the back parking lot."

"I'm walking out the door right now."

"Good. I'll…" He pulled the phone away from his ear and stared at it. She'd disconnected the call. Before he could question why she'd been so abrupt, the door on the passenger side of the car opened, and Laura slid into the seat. She glared at him, and her eyes blazed as if she were on fire. "What's wrong?" he asked.

She crossed her arms and gritted her teeth. "You tell me."

He swiveled in his seat so that he faced her and shook his head. "I can tell you're angry. I ought to know the signs. I sure saw them enough in the past, but I have no idea what's wrong this time."

She lifted her chin, and he could tell she was trying hard to keep it from trembling. "Did it slip your mind this morning to tell me about Vince?"

He narrowed his eyes and returned her angry stare.

"Oh, so that's what this is all about? You're angry because I didn't tell you when we talked this morning." He leaned closer to her and frowned. "The reason I didn't tell you is because you've had some scary things happen to you over the past few days. I thought if I could put off telling you until lunch, you'd at least have a good morning at work. Forgive me for trying to make your day better." He hoped she recognized the sarcasm in his last words.

"If you thought I was going to have a good morning, you were wrong. My river friend called right after I hung up with you, and he told me what had happened. I haven't been able to concentrate on anything all morning long."

A tear slipped from the corner of her eye, and Brad's heart lurched. She had been through a lot in the past few days and his being angry with her wasn't helping the situation a bit. He reached over and wiped the tear away with his thumb. "I'm sorry, Laura. I was going to tell you at lunch."

She stared into his eyes. "Is that the reason you asked me to have lunch with you?"

He pulled his hand back from her face and swallowed hard. "I suppose that's part of it, but there's more to it than that. I really have enjoyed being with you the past few days. I guess I wanted more time with you."

The angry lines in her face relaxed, and a sad smile pulled at her lips. "I've enjoyed it, too, Brad, but I'm also scared. We've followed two leads in my parents' case in the past few days, and both those people are dead. I don't want to be the reason for somebody else dying."

The tears streamed down her face, and Brad wished

he could give her some hope that they'd soon find the answers they were seeking. But he'd learned a long time ago that some cases were never solved. He hoped her parents' case wasn't one of those.

The best thing to do now was to take her mind off what she'd seen over the past few days. He took a deep breath and turned the ignition. "It's too hot to sit here in this car and talk. I have sandwiches and soft drinks, and I'm through testifying in court. I'm taking you to Overton Park for a picnic. We'll find the spot where we used to go and eat our lunch. For a while we'll put Tony Lynch's crime family out of our minds. It'll just be the two of us together in the middle of the park like it was when we were kids—Brad and Laura enjoying a summer day together. How would you like that?"

She smiled, and the sparkle that returned to her eyes made his pulse race. "I'd like that."

Fifteen minutes later they sat at a picnic table under a canopy of huge oak trees. A breeze rustled the leaves above, and the laughter of small children on the nearby playground drifted with it. Laura closed her eyes and smiled. "I'm glad you brought me here. This was one of our favorite places in the summer."

Brad swallowed a bite of his sandwich and nodded. "I know. I still come here sometimes on my lunch hour."

A surprised look flashed on her face. "You do?"

He nodded. "Yeah. Old habits are hard to break, I guess."

Laura stared at him without speaking for a moment, then she sighed. "I'm sorry I was angry with you earlier. I appreciate your wanting me to have a good morning. I would have, too, if that guy hadn't called."

She laid her sandwich on her napkin and propped her elbows on the table. "He knew what I was wearing today."

"What did he say?"

"He said he liked my yellow dress better than the scrubs I had on the other night." She leaned closer. "Do you think someone is watching me all the time?"

"I don't know." He let his gaze drift over the area. "I don't see anyone around here."

"It's really frightening when he calls and gives me details that he could only know if he was watching me. And then there's my telephone. Do you think we could trace his calls to me?"

"I thought of that. And I'll let our tech people take a look at it. But I'd guess that he's using a throwaway phone that can't be traced. These guys are professionals at what they do, Laura, and they wouldn't be stupid enough to use a phone that could lead the police back to them."

She nodded. "I guess you're right. So where do we go from here?"

"I've been thinking about that. Maybe we ought to skip the trip to the hospital this afternoon to see the Carsons. Instead, what do you think about our going to visit Vince's wife?"

Laura's mouth dropped open, and she blinked. "Do you think we should? The last two people we talked to ended up dead. I don't want that to happen again."

"Neither do I, but I can't let that stop me from trying to solve this case." He reached over and covered her hand with his. "Laura, there's too much at stake to give up. If I can solve your parents' case, I know it's going to lead me to Tony Lynch's crime family. I want to stop these people before they hurt some more innocent victims."

She stared at him, then put her other hand on top of his. "And I want to help you. Thank you for letting me be a part of this investigation."

He smiled. "I've always known you were smart, but you've impressed me during the time we've spent on this case. I think we work together well. I guess you could say we make a good team."

The words were no sooner out of his mouth than he regretted them. He hoped Laura didn't read more into his statement than he'd meant. If he'd used the word *professional,* Laura might have understood he didn't mean to imply there could ever be a personal relationship for them again. That had been over years ago, and they'd moved on.

Now if he kept telling himself that enough, he might eventually come to believe it himself.

The small house with its peeling paint sat on a side street not too far off a main thoroughfare through the city. Laura had never driven into this neighborhood before, and she doubted if she would want to after dark. The houses on either side of Melinda Stone's had well-kept yards, but the bars on the windows spoke volumes about the safety of the neighborhood.

Brad led the way up the front steps to the small porch and knocked on the door. Laura huddled close to him and glanced over her shoulder from time to time. There was no sound on the street except for the occasional passing car, and she wondered why there were no children playing outside.

After a repeated knock, the door cracked open. "Who is it?"

Laura stared at the chain lock that allowed the door to open only a few inches. The side of a woman's face was visible in the small crack between the door and the facing. Brad held his badge up for the woman to see. "Mrs. Stone, I'm Brad Austin with the Memphis Police Department. May I speak with you?"

"What about?"

"I saw your husband yesterday. I was sorry to hear he was killed this morning."

"Why should you care what happened to Vince?"

Brad looked over his shoulder. "Mrs. Stone, I'd like to talk to you out of the view of the whole neighborhood. Please let us come in."

She hesitated before she pushed the door closed and slid the chain lock loose. Then she opened the door and stepped back for Brad and Laura to enter. The furniture in the living room looked worn, but the room appeared neat and tidy. An open laptop sat on a desk in one corner of the room. From where Laura stood she could see a spreadsheet on the screen. She squinted in an effort to make out what it said.

Melinda walked over, closed the laptop and stared at Laura as if to accuse her of snooping. "I do bookkeeping for several companies from my home. That's how I've supported myself since Vince went to prison." She glared at Brad. "And it's all perfectly legal."

Brad nodded. "I'm not here to question you about any of your activities, Mrs. Stone."

Laura walked over to the sofa and turned back to study Mrs. Stone. At one time she probably was considered beautiful, but time had taken its toll. Wrinkles lined her face, and her short bleached hair stuck out in all directions.

The woman pointed a finger with a perfectly manicured nail toward the sofa. "Have a seat. I'd offer you something to drink, but I hope this won't take long enough to make it worth your while."

Brad shook his head. "No, ma'am. Thank you." He eased down on the sofa and pulled Laura down beside him. "As I said, I'm Detective Austin. This is Miss Laura Webber. I've been helping her with a case that concerns the murder of her parents. We went to see Vince because we thought he might be able to shed some light on that case."

The woman pulled a pack of cigarettes from her pocket and tapped one out. She was about to put it in her mouth when she looked at them and frowned. "I suppose I should ask if you mind if I smoke, but it's my house. So I guess I can smoke if I want to."

Brad nodded. "Yes, ma'am. Now back to your husband. I questioned him yesterday about the murder he was accused of committing. He claimed that he was innocent."

Melinda cocked an eyebrow and blew out a stream of smoke. "And you believed him and wanted to get him out of prison."

"No, but I listened to him."

"That's what I thought." The woman leaned forward. "But if you talked to him, you did more than anybody's done for the past twenty years. Vince was set up by somebody in Tony Lynch's family to take the fall for Johnny Sherwood's death. Vince was innocent. He tried to tell the police that, but nobody would believe him. They said his fingerprints were on the murder weapon. But he told the truth."

Brad scooted to the edge of the sofa. "How do you know that?"

Her eyes darkened. "Because I knew Vince. He never lied to me. He said he didn't do it, and I believed him." Melinda took another drag on the cigarette. "Look, Detective, I know Vince sold drugs for Tony and did maybe worse things, but he wasn't a killer. He carried a gun for protection he said, but he never used it. When he was a little boy, his father called him a sissy because he didn't like hunting. If he couldn't hurt an animal, he sure couldn't shoot a man."

Brad pulled a notepad out of his pocket and wrote something on it before he looked back at Melinda. "For the sake of argument, let's say that Vince was innocent. Why was he chosen to take the fall for whoever did it?"

Melinda reached for an ashtray on the table next to her chair and stubbed out her cigarette. "Because he was expendable."

Laura's eyes widened, and she gasped. "Why would someone think that?"

She frowned and let her gaze drift over Laura. "Miss Webber, you look like a nice young woman. You've probably always had everything you wanted and moved in circles where everybody is honest and kind. I'm here to tell you there's another world out there, and it's nothing like that."

Laura clutched her hands on her lap and nodded. "I know that, Mrs. Stone. When I was ten years old my father was a federal prosecutor who was about to take Tony Lynch to court. I watched him and my mother die when a car bomb exploded in our driveway. I learned at an early age there are people who give little thought to human life. We believe your husband was killed because he knew something about my parents' murders. That's why we went to see him yesterday."

Melinda studied her for a moment before she reached over and grasped Laura's hand. "Then we're both victims of Tony Lynch. You have my sympathy."

Tears formed in Laura's eyes. "And you have mine. I'm so sorry if our visit to your husband caused his death."

Melinda settled back in her chair and glanced at Brad. "What did you say to Vince yesterday that you think might have gotten him killed?"

She nodded from time to time as Brad recounted their conversation with Vince. He leaned forward and propped his elbows on his knees as he finished. "He wanted to get out of jail and come home, Mrs. Stone. He offered to tell what he knew about Tony's successor if the D.A. would get the two of you in the witness protection program. I wish he hadn't talked about it last night."

Melinda sighed. "Vince always talked too much. I guess it finally got him killed. He didn't give you any idea about who the successor might be?"

"No, I thought maybe you would know."

She shook her head. "I never had any contact with Tony or his men. In fact, I begged Vince all the time to get out and go back to what he loved."

"What was that?" Brad asked.

"Photography. He had a little studio that he operated part-time down on Union Avenue. At night he liked to take pictures of tourists down on Beale Street. Sometimes he'd just take pictures of whatever struck his fancy. He loved catching the bands or street musicians when they were working. He made a lot of money by taking pictures in the various clubs of people who wanted a memory of their night on the street that gave birth to the blues."

"And you wanted him to work in his studio full-time?"

She nodded. "Yes. But he said he couldn't make as much money taking pictures full-time as he could working for Tony."

"Did he take pictures in Tony's club?"

She nodded. "All the time."

"What happened to all of Vince's pictures?"

"They're in boxes in the spare bedroom. I sorted them out after Vince went to jail. I have all the ones he'd made on Beale Street right before he was arrested in a box. Would you like to see them?"

Brad nodded. "I sure would."

Melinda rose and left the room, and Brad turned to Laura. "It will be interesting to see if there are any pictures of Tony Lynch in the box."

Laura nodded. "I'm afraid to get my hopes up too much. It seems we've hit a dead end every time in the past few days."

Melinda returned carrying a large cardboard box that she set on the coffee table. "Here they are. You're welcome to take the box with you if you'd like. I don't know if there's anything inside that will help you, but I hope it will lead you to whoever killed Vince."

Brad stood and picked up the box. "I hope so, too. I'll get these back to you when I've finished going through them. In the meantime be careful. Tony's people are watching us, and they'll know we've been here."

Melinda stared at him with unblinking eyes. "I know. They're everywhere, Detective, and they don't care who they hurt. They took Vince away from me, and if I can help bring them down, I will."

Laura rose and reached for Melinda's hand. "Thank you for your help. We'll be in touch."

They walked to the front door, and Melinda opened it for them. Brad shifted the box in his arms, reached in his pocket and pulled out his card. He held it out to Melinda. "My cell phone number is on here. Call me if you think of anything else."

She stared at the card before she tucked it in the pocket of her jeans. "I will."

Laura started down the front steps but stopped on the bottom one and climbed back up to where Melinda stood. Brad glanced at her. "What are you doing?"

"I want to say something else to Melinda."

He turned and proceeded to the car with the box. Laura swallowed and fought to control her voice. "Mrs. Stone, we've both lost people in our lives whom we love, and we'll never get over that loss. I wanted to tell you one more time that I am so sorry if our visit to your husband brought about his death. I would have stayed away if I'd known that would happen. I hope you can forgive us for contributing to your loss."

Melinda's eyes filled with tears, and she reached for Laura's hand. "I'm sorry about your parents. If your father had lived, maybe he could have put a stop to Tony. But he didn't, and now those of us who have survived the horrible actions of his crime family have to try to finish what your father started. I wish you luck."

Laura put her arms around Melinda's thin shoulders and hugged her. "Thank you."

Wiping the tears from her eyes, Laura turned and hurried down the steps toward the car. Brad stood behind the car with the trunk lid raised as he slid the box inside. Laura stopped beside him and tried to smile. "That went better than I thought it would at first."

He put his hand on the top of the trunk lid to close it and smiled. "Yeah. Maybe we made some progress tonight."

Laura nodded and walked around the car to the passenger door. Behind her she heard the sound of an approaching vehicle, and she stepped closer to their car so that she was out of the way.

Suddenly the trunk banged closed, and Brad screamed. "Laura! Watch out!"

Before she could react, Brad's body slammed into her and knocked her forward. They both landed facedown on the paved street just as shots rang out above them. Glass shattered and pelted down on top of them. A scream near the house pierced the early evening air.

Brad's body covered hers, and his hand pushed her head down onto the street's surface. The driver of the shooter's car accelerated, and the vehicle roared down the street. At the corner, the tires squealed, and Brad loosened his hold on Laura.

He sat up and pulled her into a sitting position. His hands gripped her arms, but she could feel them trembling. "Laura, are you all right?"

She rubbed her head where she'd scraped it on the pavement and nodded. "I think so."

He jumped to his feet and pulled her up just as Melinda Stone appeared next to them. "Are you two okay?"

"We are, thanks to Brad," Laura said. "How did you know there was a shooter in that car?"

He rubbed his hand through his hair, and shards of the shattered window glass fell to the ground. "I had just turned from closing the trunk when I spotted the car. They were passing a streetlamp, and I guess the light reflected off the barrel. I just caught a glimpse of it before I tackled you. I hope I didn't hurt you."

Laura shook her head. "Hurt me? Brad, you saved my life. How can I ever thank you for that?"

His gaze raked her face, and a warm feeling surged through her veins. "It's my job, Laura. I'm glad I was here with you." He reached for the door handle and opened the car door. More glass fell to the ground, and he reached inside and brushed some out of the seat. "I'd better get you home now. It's been another unsettling day for you."

Laura watched as he walked around the car and climbed in on the driver's side before she smiled at Melinda. "I'm glad you weren't hurt, either. Take care of yourself."

"I will. Come back anytime."

As soon as Laura had shut her door, Brad started the engine and pulled away from the curb. He didn't speak as they drove through the city, except to tell Laura they'd have to go to dinner some other night. When they reached Charles and Nora's house, he stopped in front and turned off the motor. He didn't speak for a moment.

"Laura, this is getting way too dangerous for you. I don't think you should go back to work for a while."

Laura took a deep breath. "I know you're trying to protect me, but I can't let these people win. I have clients who need my help, and I need to be there for them."

He raked his hand through his hair. "I knew you would say that, but I don't want something to happen to you."

"I know you don't. I suppose I'm going to have to be more aware of my surroundings from now on. Charles will follow me to work tomorrow."

"If you want me to, I'll come after work."

"I'd like that."

He straightened behind the wheel and inhaled. "Then I guess I'll see you tomorrow."

She smiled and opened the car door. "I hope you can get your car fixed without too much trouble."

"I'm just glad it's my car and not you." He waited for her to close the door before he put the car in gear and drove down the driveway.

Laura hurried to the front porch and watched as he pulled into the street. Brad had seemed very upset over the shooting incident. She was, too, but it seemed to have affected him much worse. She hoped he didn't blame himself for letting her go along on his investigation.

Even though she'd been terrified when those bullets had sailed over her head, she had felt safe because Brad's arms were around her. She hadn't felt like that since she'd left him six years ago, and she'd missed that feeling.

But she had to be honest with herself. She'd thrown away a beautiful relationship when she left, and she wasn't likely to ever recover it.

NINE

Brad poured another cup of coffee and sat back down at the kitchen table. He'd been up for hours going through the pictures Melinda Stone had given him the night before, but so far he'd found nothing. Truthfully, though, he had no idea what he was even looking for. He kept telling himself he'd know when he saw it. He sure hoped so. This was getting him nowhere fast. He set aside the last stack he'd looked through and took a sip from his cup. He frowned as he pulled some more from the box. Who were all these people, and where had they come from? So far he hadn't recognized anyone.

Most of the people in the photographs looked like tourists who'd posed while having a good time in one of the clubs. Then there were the musicians and acrobats who'd been caught on film performing in the middle of the street. He wondered if Vince had made as much money as Melinda thought if this many pictures hadn't been purchased.

Brad shook his head and continued to sort through the ones he'd just pulled from the box. Some he placed in a stack to reexamine later, and others he discarded. He was about to toss one aside when he stopped and picked it up again. He squinted and held it closer to his eyes for a better look.

On the surface the picture appeared to be a group enjoying a birthday party, but closer inspection revealed much more than Brad had first realized. From the posters and music symbols on the wall behind the group, he knew the picture had been taken inside one of the clubs on Beale Street. A man holding a knife, seated at a round table, smiled at the camera as he prepared to cut the birthday cake in front of him. Two men flanked him, and eight more stood behind.

Brad had never met the man in person, but he'd seen enough pictures during his time on the force to recognize the man with the knife—Tony Lynch. Brad turned the picture over, and read the writing on the back. *Tony Lynch and guests at his birthday party, March 7, 1993.*

Brad didn't think he'd ever seen the other men in the picture before, but he couldn't be sure. After all, they'd aged since that photograph was taken and probably looked nothing like they did then.

He jumped up from the table, hurried to his desk in the bedroom, and pulled out the top drawer. The magnifying glass he used sometimes lay inside, and he grabbed it. Back in the kitchen, he held the glass close to the picture and studied each individual's face. He still didn't recognize anybody. He was about to lay the photo aside when he moved the glass over the form of a young man standing behind one of the men in the chair.

Something about him looked familiar, but Brad couldn't decide what it was. He held the glass still and concentrated on the young face. Where had he seen this man before?

Suddenly it came to him. He'd encountered the man, now twenty years older, at the fund-raiser for the homeless shelter he'd attended last winter. Before the evening was over the man had donated a large sum of money to the shelter, which had surprised no one. He was one of the biggest charity donors in the county, or at least that's what he'd told Charles when they'd been discussing Lucas Pennington.

Charles had said that Lucas attended every day of Vince Stone's trial. Now there he was in a picture taken before the Webbers' deaths at a birthday party for the man suspected of ordering the hits.

Brad reached for his cell phone and punched in a number. When it rang several times with no answer, he started to disconnect, but a groggy voice finally answered. "Hello?"

Brad smiled and glanced at his watch. "Aren't you out of bed yet?"

A growl rumbled in his ear. "Is that you, Austin? Why are you calling so early in the morning?"

"It's not that early. I need a favor."

"Okay, okay. Give me time to collect my thoughts here. I was up nearly all night working on that new computer program I'm developing." Brad heard a bed creak. "I'm sittin' up now. What do you want besides saying thank-you for the information I gathered for you on Sylvia Warner?"

"I really do appreciate that, Thompson. You helped me find her all right. The trouble was it led somebody else there. She was murdered that night."

"Oh, man, that's awful."

"Yeah, well, I'm still on the case, and I need you to do some more research for me."

He suppressed a smile when he heard his friend's long sigh. "All right, Austin. What do you need me to do now?"

"I need some information on Lucas Pennington."

"The lawyer?"

"Yeah. I need to know if there's a record of a connection between him and Tony Lynch."

"What kind of connection?"

"Anything. Has Pennington ever represented Lynch or any of his employees? Do they own property together? Are they partners in a business? I need to find a link between the two."

"This is not something I can do in a few hours. It's going to take some time. I'll let you know if I find anything."

"Good. And thanks for helping me out. I owe you."

"Always glad to do it. I'll be in touch."

Brad disconnected the call and sat there thinking about the conversation. He'd read a few years ago that people had no idea how many digital footprints they left every day. Rick Thompson was just the guy to find whatever tracks Lucas Pennington had left behind.

Maybe things were beginning to come together in this case. With the kind of business dealings Tony Lynch had, he would only have close friends and associates at his birthday party. Lucas Pennington had to have a close tie to be there.

Brad's pulse raced at the thought that he might have just unearthed the best clue he'd had so far in this case. Perhaps it was time he paid a visit to one of Memphis's most prominent attorneys and asked him about his connection to Tony Lynch. The answer should be very interesting.

* * *

Brad stepped off the elevator right into the large waiting room of Pennington and Associates law firm. When he'd called to tell his partners where he was going, Alex had told him that the law firm took up the whole third floor of the building where it was housed on Front Street. He wondered if the waiting room with its comfortable sofas and chairs covered half of that area.

A young woman sat behind the receptionist's desk at the side of the room, and she looked up and smiled as he approached. "May I help you?"

Brad pulled out his badge and held it up. "I'm Detective Austin with the Memphis Police Department. I called earlier about meeting with Mr. Pennington."

She smiled and pointed to one of the chairs. "Yes. Please have a seat, and I'll let Mr. Pennington know you're here."

"Thank you."

Brad ambled over to the wingback chair next to a table with magazines and newspapers stacked on top and had a seat. He picked up the morning copy of *The Commercial Appeal* and opened it to the sports page. He'd just finished reading about the St. Louis Cardinals' game the night before when he heard his name being called.

He glanced up at the receptionist. "Mr. Pennington will see you now. Go down the hallway to the right of this room, and his office is the last one on the left."

Brad nodded and headed in the direction she'd indicated. As he walked down the hallway, he noticed several of the office doors stood ajar, but he didn't see anyone inside. He stopped at the one with the name-plate that had Pennington in bold letters and knocked.

"Come in."

Lucas Pennington rose from behind his desk as Brad walked in the room. Lucas smiled and extended his hand. "Detective Austin?"

Brad nodded and shook the man's hand. "Yes."

Lucas motioned for Brad to sit in the chair in front of his desk and returned to his seat. He leaned forward, rested his arms on his desk and laced his fingers together. "How can I help you this morning, Detective?"

Brad pulled the photo from his pocket and slid it across Lucas's desk. "I'm working on a cold case that I believe is linked to the Tony Lynch crime family, and I came across this photograph. I wondered what you can tell me about it."

Lucas stared at the picture for a few moments before he smiled. "This picture must be over twenty years old. I was in school at the University of Memphis then."

"Twenty years is about right," Brad said. "The date's on the back. But I'd like to know what your connection to Lynch was. You must have been good friends to be at his birthday party."

Lucas shook his head. "No. I hardly knew the man."

Brad's eyebrows arched. "Do you expect me to believe that you are in a picture with Tony Lynch, the head of the biggest crime organization in the South, and some of his hired thugs and that you barely knew him? That makes no sense whatsoever."

Lucas tossed the picture across the desk to Brad and leaned back in his chair. "It's the truth. When I came to college, I was on a scholarship and had to find a job to help pay my expenses. Mr. Lynch gave me a job as a janitor at his club on Beale Street. I worked every night and on weekends. I knew nothing about any of his illegal activities until years later. I thought he made a living from his club. He was good to me and paid me well."

"And he invited you to his birthday party because you were one of his employees?"

Lucas's face turned red, and he shifted in his chair. "I wasn't invited to the party. I was cleaning the night that was taken. He saw me and invited me to have a piece of cake. The picture was snapped right before he cut the cake."

Brad regarded him with a skeptical stare before he spoke again. "I suppose you were working at the club when Johnny Sherwood was killed."

He nodded. "I was."

"Were you working there when Lawrence and Madeline Webber were killed by a car bomb?"

Lucas frowned and leaned forward. "Wait a minute. Are you here because you think I might have had something to do with those murders?"

Brad shrugged. "Well, did you? You attended the trial of Vince Stone every day."

Lucas jumped to his feet and pounded his fist on his desk. "I was a college kid when the Webbers were killed. I heard about it because that's all that was on the news for weeks. I had nothing to do with that. The reason I went to Vince Stone's trial was because I was going to be starting law school in the fall, and I wanted to follow a high profile trial. There was no other reason."

Brad pushed to his feet, picked up the picture from the desk and slipped it in his pocket. "So let me see if I've got this all right. You worked for Tony Lynch when you were in college, and you liked him because he was good to you. He knew you were going to law school at the same time he was looking for someone to succeed him as head of his organization. You went to Vince Stone's trial because it was high profile and never gave it a thought that Johnny Sherwood's murder was connected to the Webbers."

Lucas raised a shaking hand and pointed a finger at Brad. "You'd better think twice before you accuse me of anything."

Brad shook his head. "I'm not accusing you of anything, Mr. Pennington. I'm just trying to get it all straight in my head."

Lucas walked to the door and put his hand on the knob. "I think you've taken up enough of my time, Detective. It's time for you to go."

Brad sauntered to the door and stopped facing Lucas. "There's just one more thing I'd like to ask you. After you became a lawyer, did you ever represent Tony Lynch in any legal matters?"

Lucas's eyes narrowed, and his nostrils flared. "You're smart enough to know that whomever I represent is privileged information, and I can't reveal any names to you."

Brad exhaled and nodded. "No, I guess you can't do that, but let me give you a friendly warning. I'm going to bring Tony Lynch's organization down. If in the course of my investigation I find even the tiniest hint that you may be involved with him, I'll have the feds in here with a search warrant so fast it'll make your head spin."

Lucas glared at him. "Bring it on, Detective. I don't have anything to hide."

"I hope not for your sake, Mr. Pennington."

Lucas opened the door, and Brad walked out without a backward glance. Lucas Pennington could bear watching. Something told him that the lawyer who'd donated millions to charities in the area had a secret, and he intended to find out what it was.

Laura's cell phone had been silent all morning. She'd expected Brad to call and ask how she was feeling after almost getting killed at Melinda Stone's house last night, but so far she hadn't heard from him. She picked the phone up from her desk and stared at it. Maybe she should call him.

She punched in the first two digits of his number and then paused. What was she doing? Brad knew her phone number. If he wanted to check on her, he would call. She didn't need to give him the idea she was getting too attached to him.

A knock at the door jerked her from her thoughts, and she laid the phone down. "Come in."

The door opened, and Josh stuck his head around the side. "Are you busy?"

"No. Did you need something?"

He pushed the door all the way open, walked in and plopped down in the chair across from her desk. Dark circles lined his eyes, and he looked as if he hadn't slept in days. The shadow of a beard gave him a scruffy look, and she frowned. She'd never seen him look so disheveled before.

"Is something wrong, Josh?"

He grimaced and rubbed the back of his neck.

"Yeah. I thought you'd probably heard from one of the other nurses by now."

Laura shook her head. "No, I haven't talked to anybody since I came in this morning. What happened?"

"When I got home from work yesterday, my dad called and said that the house where I grew up had burned while he and Mom were at work. They lost everything." He rubbed his hands over his eyes. "I can't believe this. My folks are homeless right now with only the clothes that they were wearing."

Laura's heart pricked at the sorrow on Josh's face. "I'm so sorry. What are they going to do?"

Josh exhaled a deep breath and pushed to his feet. "They're staying with my aunt and uncle right now, and they said several community agencies were helping them. They're back to like they were when they first married. They have nothing but each other, and I'm five hundred miles away. I feel like I need to go home and help them, but they don't want me to come. They're so proud that I finished nursing school and have a good job."

Laura rose from her chair and walked around the desk. She stopped in front of him. "I know this is a difficult time for you, Josh. Remember that I'm your friend, and I'm here for you if you'd like to talk."

He smiled a sad smile and nodded. "Thanks, Laura. I've felt closer to you than anyone else since I started working here. I guess I'm feeling guilty that I'm not there with them."

She shook her head. "You shouldn't feel that way. You're doing what your parents want. You're living the life they wanted you to have. And don't think of them as not having anything. They have each other, and that's the most important thing right now. They're safe, and they love you. I'm sure they'll get through this fine."

His gaze drifted over her face. "I appreciate your talking to me. I think I feel better already."

The sadness that flickered in his eyes reminded her of how her brother, Mark, had looked at times after their parents' deaths. He had wanted someone to comfort him then, and she had always been the one to do it.

She reached up, wrapped her arms around Josh's neck and gave him a hug. His body stiffened for a moment, and then his arms encircled her. His breath fanned the side of her face as he whispered in her ear, "Oh, Laura, you're so sweet."

Laura realized too late that the comforting hug she'd intended for Josh had turned into something quite different. She loosened her arms from around his neck, but he only drew her closer. "Josh, you can't…"

"Excuse me. I hope I'm not interrupting anything."

The harsh words felt like a slap, and Laura pushed free of Josh. She stared past him to the open door where she spied Brad. His open stance and clenched fists at his side intensified the anger she saw flashing in his dark eyes.

"B-Brad," she mumbled. "What are you doing here?"

"I came by to check on you." His burning stare darted from her to Josh who had now turned to face him.

Laura pushed a stray lock of hair behind her ear and took a step away from Josh. She swallowed and tried to speak. "Brad, this is Josh Nelson. He's a nurse here at the clinic." She glanced at Josh. "And this is Detective Brad Austin of the Memphis Police Department."

Josh walked over to Brad and stuck out his hand. "Nice to meet you, Detective."

The muscle in Brad's face twitched, but he shook Josh's hand. "You, too."

Laura's nostrils flared at the sudden chilly atmosphere in the room. She crossed her arms and hugged them close to her body. "Do you need to speak with me, Brad?"

"For a few minutes." He glanced at Josh. "Then I'll get out of your way."

Josh backed toward the hallway. "I'll catch you later, Laura. And thanks for all your help."

"You're welcome, Josh."

Brad looked over his shoulder as Josh walked down the hall and then turned to face her. "Is this a bad time for you?"

"No. Close the door and have a seat."

Her knees trembled as she walked back around her desk and sat down. She tried to smile as Brad settled himself in the chair where Josh had sat minutes ago. Laura's heart raced as Brad leaned back and sighed. "You haven't mentioned your friend."

Her face burned under his probing stare, and she fidgeted in her seat. "There's nothing to tell. Josh graduated from nursing school last year, and he started working here soon after I did. We're friends. Nothing more."

A sneer pulled at Brad's lips. "Yeah, mighty good friends, I'd say."

His words hit her like sharp barbs, and she bristled. "I'd say he's a good friend. His parents' home burned last night, and I was trying to comfort him." She felt her anger rising, and she halted before she said something she would regret. Brad might have had the right to question her actions years ago, but he didn't now. He had let her know from the beginning that he didn't want to renew their relationship. She took a deep breath and lifted her chin.

"I'm sure you have female friends that I'm not aware of, and that's the way it should be. We gave up the right to care about each other's life years ago."

There was no change in his stoic expression. He simply nodded. "You're right. I shouldn't have questioned you. It doesn't matter to me anyway." He took a deep breath. "The reason I came by was to tell you about my meeting this morning with Lucas Pennington."

Laura clutched her trembling hands on her lap and tried to appear interested as Brad related what had happened at Lucas Pennington's officer earlier, but his words barely registered. All she could think about was that he had said it didn't matter to him who her friends were. In other words, he had let her know that his feelings for her had died, and they would never return. She struggled to hold back the tears and to appear like she was listening.

When he finished, he pushed to his feet. "That's all I wanted to tell you. I think that Pennington has some link to your parents' deaths, but I don't know what it is yet."

She stood. "I'm sure you'll find it, Brad."

"I hope so." He glanced at his watch. "It's later than I thought. I need to get to the office. My partners and

I are scheduled to look at another cold case this morning."

"Good luck with that one."

"Thank you." He walked to the door but turned before he left the office. "Oh, by the way, do you think Charles could come by and follow you home today?"

She nodded. "I'm sure he could."

"Good. I'm going to be tied up and won't have time to do that. I suggest you don't go anywhere tonight. After last night, I think you should take extra precautions."

She tried to smile. "I'll do that. When will I see you again?"

He shrugged. "I don't know. I may have to ask Alex or Seth to take over for me where you're concerned. I have so much on my plate right now I can't get it all done."

She straightened her shoulders and nodded. "I understand, Brad. Thank you for all you've done on my parents' case so far."

He stared at her for a moment, and she had the horrible thought that this might be the last time she'd see him for a while. "Like I told you at the beginning, Laura—it's my job. That's all it is—a job."

Before she could respond, he strode from the room. She listened to his footsteps recede down the hallway before she dropped back down in her chair and began to sob. For the past few days she had thought she and Brad might be on their way back to finding each other again. Now that hope had vanished, and once again she had the same feeling that had haunted her for years after her parents' deaths. She was alone, and there was nothing she could do about it.

TEN

Brad stormed into his office, grunted as he strode past a surprised Alex and Seth and dropped down in his desk chair. He slammed the notebook he'd been carrying onto the top of his desk and jerked a drawer open. He fumbled inside the drawer but couldn't find the report he'd been working on the day before.

With a growl he slammed the drawer shut and looked up to see his two partners standing at the entrance to his cubicle. He looked from one to the other. "What?"

"You tell us, buddy," Alex said. "You're acting like a wild man. What happened?"

"Nothing happened. I'm just on edge this morning."

Seth nodded. "We can see that. Anything we can do to help?"

"No. I just need some space."

Alex glanced at Seth. "Okay, we can do that. Let me know if there's anything I can do to help."

Brad pushed to his feet. "There's nothing anybody can do to help," he muttered. "Maybe a cup of coffee will make me feel better."

He pushed past his two friends and headed down the hallway to the break room. He stopped outside the door to let two officers exit with their coffee before he entered the area that offered a few minutes of refuge from an officer's busy day. When he stepped inside and pulled a cup from the shelf, his mood took another nosedive at the sight of an empty coffeepot.

He stood there a minute staring at the empty pot before he put the cup back on the shelf and sat down on the sofa. He propped his elbows on his knees and buried his face in his hands. What was the matter with him? He'd acted like a toddler having a tantrum and had been rude to his partners. They didn't deserve his foul attitude today.

Laura didn't deserve it, either. They'd been honest from the very beginning about how they couldn't go back to what they once had. It wasn't her fault that he had decided he wanted to go back. In fact that's all he thought about—having her back in his life. The awful truth was that he had never quit loving her, but it wasn't going to get him anywhere now, just as it hadn't six years ago. It was evident she didn't return his feelings.

He heard footsteps enter the room, and he looked up to see Alex standing in front of him. His hands were stuck in his pockets, and he stared down at Brad. "I thought I'd check on you."

Brad took a deep breath. "Thanks."

"It's Laura, isn't it?"

He nodded. "Yeah. How did you guess?"

Alex eased down on the couch beside him. "It wasn't hard. You're acting just like you did when she left. She's gotten under your skin again."

Brad shook his head. "I don't think I ever got rid of her. I've told myself I was over her, but I've always known she was the only one for me. The problem is, she doesn't feel the same way."

"I'm sorry to hear that. Did something happen?"

Brad chuckled. "I guess you could say that. I walked into her office and found her in the arms of another man."

Alex frowned. "Oh, man, that's gotta be tough. Did she say anything?"

"She said he was a friend, a fellow nurse who worked with her, and that his parents' house burned yesterday. She was trying to comfort him."

"But you didn't believe her?"

"No, why should I? She had her arms around the guy's neck."

Alex shrugged. "I'm only asking because Laura never struck me as a person who lies. I guess it surprises me that she would."

Brad frowned and straightened. "Hold on a minute. I never said Laura is a liar."

"Well, you said you didn't believe her. What else am I to think?"

Brad raked his hand through his hair and gritted his teeth. "I don't know." He glanced at Alex who was smiling, and his shoulders relaxed. "That's your way of telling me I overreacted, isn't it?"

"I'd say so. We've both known Laura since high school, and we know she tells the truth. If she said this guy's a friend, you ought to believe her."

A sheepish smile pulled at Brad's mouth. "Thanks for setting me straight. I feel better now."

Alex tilted his head to one side and directed a steady gaze at Brad. "I hate to see you getting tied up in knots over Laura again. Be careful this time."

"I will. I'm not sure if Laura and I can ever go back to where we were."

"Maybe you don't need to go back. Maybe you need to start over. You've been apart six years, and you've both changed. Get to know her again, and let her get to know you before you make any decisions about the future."

Brad swallowed hard and shook his head. "Thanks for being a good friend. You always seem to know what to say to make me see things clearer."

Alex laughed and pushed to his feet. "I've had enough experience through the years. Like I said, just take it slow."

"I will."

Brad sat on the sofa a few more minutes after Alex left, and then he pulled out his phone and dialed Laura's number. She answered right away. "Hello."

"Laura, it's Brad."

"I know. Your name came up on caller ID. Is there something you need?"

The cool tone of her voice sent a chill through him. He closed his eyes and swallowed. "I called to apologize for the way I acted at your office. I'm afraid I came across as rude. I wasn't very nice to your friend."

"Oh? So you're really calling to tell me you're sorry for being rude to Josh."

"No, that's not…" He hesitated and took a deep breath. "I'm sorry for the way I acted toward you. When I walked in and saw you in that guy's arms, I guess I overreacted."

"Brad, I told you what had happened. The house he grew up in burned to the ground. His parents lost everything they have, and he's worried about them. I wanted to let him know I was here for him, but there's nothing going on between us other than friendship."

"You don't have to explain to me. It's really none of my business, but I'd like to make it up to you for my nasty behavior earlier."

"And how do you propose to do that?"

"I know I told you to stay inside, but maybe we could grab an early dinner tonight. I could pick you up at the clinic when it closes, and we could go to some place that attracts a large crowd. I'd feel safer having you in a large group than our being alone."

He held his breath while he waited for her answer. "Charles followed me to work this morning, so my car is in the parking lot."

"We'll leave it there while we eat. Then I'll take you back to get it and follow you home. How's that?"

"I think that sounds great. I'll be finished here a little before six tonight."

"I'll be waiting in the back parking lot." He paused and licked his lips. "And thanks for being so understanding, Laura. I really am sorry about earlier."

A soft sigh rippled over the phone. "I'm sure your reaction was triggered by what happened in the past between us. I'm sorry for what I put you through. I'd do things very differently if I had the chance to go back. But we can't undo the past, can we?"

He closed his eyes and bit down on his lip. "No, we can't. All we can do is try to change our behavior. I'll try not to overreact in the future."

"And I'll try to be more aware of your feelings. I wasn't always, and I'm truly sorry for that."

He took a deep breath. "I'll see you about six."

"I'm already looking forward to it."

He disconnected the call and stared at the phone as he recalled the conversation. The tone of her voice had been different after he apologized. It reminded him of how she'd sounded years ago when they would sit for hours and talk about the future and what they wanted to do. Even her words hinted at a sorrow about what had happened between them.

For the first time since he'd discovered Laura sitting at his desk, he began to have hope that they might be able to resolve the past and move toward the future together. In his heart he knew that's what he wanted. Did he dare hope she felt the same way? Time would tell.

Laura glanced around at the crowded restaurant and shook her head in dismay. There wasn't another woman in the place who had come to dinner straight from work. She looked down at the rumpled skirt and blouse she'd worn today and frowned.

Brad stopped cutting his steak and laid his knife and fork on his plate. "What's the matter? Don't you like your food?"

Laura blinked and directed her attention back to him. "Of course I like my food."

"But you've hardly touched it."

She leaned forward and lowered her voice. "Brad, look at the other people in this place. I'm sure none of these women wore the clothes they have on now to work today. In fact I'd bet most of them didn't even go to work today. This is one of the most exclusive restaurants in town. I thought it was almost impossible to get a reservation here."

He shrugged and rolled his eyes. "I don't know

about that. I just called and told them what time we'd be here."

"You just called? That's all?"

His face turned crimson, and he took a drink of water. "Well, I might have asked to speak to the owner. I got to know him when I investigated a case a few years ago."

She sat back in her seat, crossed her arms and grinned. "Detective Austin, I can't believe you used your influence to get us into the swankiest restaurant in town."

He returned her smile and picked up his fork. "It may be a ritzy place, but I eat here a lot. I like the food, and I like the people who work here. I call and order dinner from here and pick it up on my way home."

She picked up her water glass and let her gaze drift over the ornate ceilings with the beautiful crown moldings and the elegantly draped tables with flickering candles. "Well, you know how to impress a girl."

He pointed to her plate with his fork. "You can impress me by eating your dinner. With what I'm paying for that, I don't want to see a bite left."

She laughed and stuck a bite of chicken in her mouth. "Um, that's good. See, I'm eating my dinner, Detective Austin."

He cocked an eyebrow and shook his head. "Don't be funny. Just eat."

She started to respond, but a voice interrupted her. "Brad, it's good to see you."

"Hi, Jimmy. I didn't think you were here tonight."

Laura looked up at the middle-aged man who stood beside their table. "I hadn't planned to work tonight, but I dropped by for a minute." He glanced down at

Laura, and his dark eyes lit up. "And I must say it's good to see you with somebody for a change and not taking your dinner home to eat alone. Aren't you going to introduce me to your lovely dinner companion?"

Brad laid his napkin beside his plate and smiled. "Jimmy, this is Laura Webber, an old friend of mine. Laura, this is Jimmy Curtis. He owns this restaurant."

Laura smiled and extended her hand. "I'm so glad to meet you, Mr. Curtis. This is my first time in your restaurant, and everything is delicious."

He took her hand in both of his and squeezed. "I'm glad you're enjoying your meal. So, you're an old friend of Brad's?"

"Yes, we went to high school and college together. I've been away from Memphis for a while, but I've recently moved back."

His eyebrows arched, and he glanced at Brad. "Ah, I see. Then maybe Brad will bring you here more often. All he has to do is let me know he's coming, and I'll have one of our best tables ready for him."

Laura cast a questioning glance at Brad. "That's very kind of you. Have you known Brad for a long time?"

Mr. Curtis stepped closer to Brad and placed his hand on his shoulder. "This man gave me back my son. When he was accused of murdering a classmate, Brad thought he'd been set up. He didn't give up until he'd found the real killer and proved my son was innocent. My wife and I will always be grateful to him."

Brad fidgeted in his chair, and his face grew red. "I've told you over and over, I was just doing my job."

Mr. Curtis shook his head. "No, my friend. You went way beyond what your job required because you wanted to help a boy you believed was innocent. My wife and I thank God every day that you were the detective assigned to investigate that murder. God used you to bring our son home." He turned and looked at Laura. "What do you think about that?"

"I'm not surprised at all. Brad isn't only a good policeman, he's a good man. I've always known that."

"And so do I, Miss Webber." He glanced at his watch. "I have to go. My wife and son are waiting at home for me. We're going to a play at the Orpheum. I'll tell your waiter on the way out that dessert is on the house tonight. Enjoy your meal, and I hope to see you in here again soon."

Neither of them spoke as they watched Mr. Curtis walk across the dining room toward the kitchen door. When the door closed behind him, Brad picked up his knife and fork, cut a bit of steak and popped it in his mouth. He paused in chewing when he looked across the table and noticed Laura staring at him. He swallowed and frowned. "What?"

"You have quite a fan in Mr. Curtis. No wonder you eat here a lot if you get the royal treatment all the time."

"I wouldn't call him a fan. He's a nice guy, and he appreciates what I did for his son."

"It goes beyond appreciation, Brad. He cares about you enough to pray for you every day. It's a great blessing to have someone who does that for you."

"I never thought of it that way." Brad waved his hand in dismissal and shook his head. "Like I told him, I was only doing my job."

The remark reminded her he'd said the same thing to her recently. A pang of regret pierced her heart, and she winced. "Like you are with me?"

He speared another piece of steak and had his fork halfway to his mouth when she spoke. He paused and lowered the fork slowly. He stared at his plate a moment before he looked up. "No, Laura, with you it's different. It's more than a job."

His gaze didn't waver from hers, and her pulse raced. For the first time she felt as if they might be on their way to restoring what they'd lost years ago. Did she dare push him to find out? She took a deep breath.

"Mr. Curtis is not the only one who prays for you every day, Brad. I do, too. I've prayed for you every day since I left Memphis. I've asked God to keep you safe in your job and to give you a happy life. And I've asked Him to help you forgive me."

"Do we have to go into this now?"

"I think we do. After what happened in my office this morning, I had convinced myself you still hated me. Then you called and apologized and invited me to dinner. That gave me reason to hope that you have forgiven me for how I hurt you. But I'm confused. One minute I think we will never be friends again, and the next I think we've made a lot of progress."

He sighed and rubbed his hand over his eyes. "I've spent the past six years telling myself that I hate you. Then you reappear in my life, and all the old memories start to stir. I could never hate you, Laura. We have too much history for that."

"I'm glad to hear you say that. I've missed having you in my life."

"I've missed you, too."

"Maybe we can use our good memories to help us rebuild our friendship in the future."

He smiled. "I'd like that. I'd like that a lot."

* * *

Laura dropped down in her desk chair and blew at a lock of hair that dangled on her forehead. From the minute she'd gotten to work this morning she'd been faced with one task after another. Now having finished an especially grueling counseling session with the parents of a teenage boy who was killed in a drive-by shooting, she needed to relax for a few minutes and try to calm her emotions. Maybe a cup of coffee would help, but she only had thirty minutes before her group counseling session.

A knock sounded at the door, and she groaned. What now?

"Come in." She tried to sound cheerier than what she felt.

The door opened, and Josh stuck his head in the door. He looked better this morning than he had yesterday, but his eyes were still bloodshot. "Are you busy?"

She shook her head. "No, I'm just taking a few minutes before my next session. Have a seat."

He dropped down in the chair and stretched his legs out in front of him. "I need a few minutes, too. Dr. Jones has seen one patient after another this morning. It's been like a revolving door in the exam rooms."

She studied him for a moment. "How are things going with your parents?"

"Better. The insurance company is working with them. Maybe they'll know something soon. In the meantime they're going to stay at my aunt and uncle's house until they can find a small apartment. Mom sounds real upbeat. She says it reminds her of their college days when they were first married and had nothing."

Laura smiled. "It sounds like she has a good attitude about the fire."

"Yeah, but my dad's a different story. He's really down over losing everything. Mom says for me not to worry, but I can't help it. I feel like I should be there."

"I'm sure they want you…" The ringing of her cell phone interrupted her, and she pulled it from her pants pocket. "Hello."

"I thought I'd check in and see how you are this morning."

The low rumble of the voice she'd first heard when she was awakened after her kidnapping sent shivers down her spine. "W-what do you want?"

"Nothing other than to hear your sweet voice. I like to hear that hint of fear when you realize who's calling."

"Well, see how you like this." She pulled the phone away from her ear and disconnected the call. She glanced up to see Josh staring at her with a confused expression.

"I don't mean to pry, but you look upset. Who was that on the phone?"

"Nobody of importance." She reached for a stack of papers on the edge of her desk, but her hand trembled so she could hardly pick them up. "I need to get ready for my next session."

Josh stood. "Then I'd better get out of here."

At that moment Lucy Watkins, the director of nursing at the clinic, stuck her head in the door. "Laura, the garbage truck is here to empty the Dumpster. The driver says your car is parked so close to it he can't get the truck in position to lift it. Can you go move your car?"

Laura jumped to her feet. "Oh, I'm sorry. I was running late this morning, and all the parking spaces were taken. I had to park there, but I meant to go back and move it later. I'll do it right now."

She grabbed her purse and began to dig inside, but she couldn't find the keys. Josh glanced back before stepping into the hall. An amused expression covered his face. "Is something wrong?"

"I can't find my keys." She stopped rummaging in her purse and tried to remember what she'd done earlier when she came to work. The answer hit her, and she pulled her keys out of her pants pocket. "Here they are."

"Glad you found them." With a laugh, Josh turned and headed down the hall.

Laura clutched her keys and hurried toward the exit. Right before she reached the door, Lucy stepped out of a room at the end of the hallway and turned toward the exit door. She carried a cardboard box in her hands.

Laura caught up with her at the door. "Are you leaving?"

Lucy nodded. "I'm taking the rest of the day off, and I offered to take this box of books by the accountant's office on my way home. The office is short staffed today, and it's right on my way."

Laura held the door for Lucy to exit and then followed her across the parking lot to her car. "Let me get that door for you." She opened the car door and stepped back as Lucy slid the box into the backseat.

"Thanks, Laura. I appreciate it. I'll see you tomorrow." She started to get in the car, but she stopped and turned back to Laura. "Dr. Jones told me you've had some bad things going on in your life lately. I wanted you to know I'm thinking about you and praying for you."

"I appreciate that." Laura took a deep breath. "I'm just trying to be as careful as I can."

"You take care." Lucy cranked the engine and backed from her parking place.

Laura watched her pull away and then turned toward the garbage truck. It sat in the middle of the drive with its motor idling. A man in a hard hat stood beside the truck. He scowled at her. "If you're through socializing, lady, I'd really like for you to move your car."

She flinched at the angry look on his face and walked over to him. "I'm so sorry, sir. I don't make a habit of parking here, and I meant to move my car. But it's been a busy morning. I got tied up and forgot."

He glanced down at his watch. "Well, you're here now. Could you hurry up and move it? I'm already behind schedule."

She tried to muster up the most contrite expression she could. "I'll do it right away." He didn't look like he was buying her excuse. She turned toward her car.

Before she could take a step, a deafening sound split the air, and her car exploded in a ball of flames. The blast knocked Laura and the sanitation worker off their feet, and debris and chunks of metal rained down all around.

Stunned but conscious, Laura lay on the ground. Panicked voices echoed across the lot as the employees of the clinic poured into the parking lot. She looked up to see Josh peering down at her.

"Laura, are you all right?"

She tried to sit up, but he pushed her back down. "Yes, I'm okay. How about the truck driver?"

Josh glanced past her and shook his head. "I don't know. They're checking him now. We've called 911. The police and ambulances should be here any minute. You don't have any apparent injuries, but we need to get you to the hospital and rule out any internal ones. Be still until we can get you there."

She closed her eyes and shivered at the memory of her caller's voice. He'd known what was going to happen, and he'd called to taunt her. If she'd had any idea what her appearance on television would cause, she wouldn't have done the interview. Now instead of dealing with the memory of one car exploding in flames, she had two to remember. She didn't know how she was going to be able to do that.

When would this nightmare end?

ELEVEN

All morning Brad had looked through the pictures he'd taken from Melinda Stone's house a few nights ago. There were no more photographs of Lucas Pennington, and he had no idea what his next step with the attorney would be.

The door to the office opened, and Alex and Seth strolled in. Each held a fast food paper bag. He leaned back in his chair and stretched.

"Where have you guys been this morning?"

Alex set his bag down on his desk and walked over to Brad's cubicle. "We went to the hospital to see how Nathan Carson is doing. He hasn't regained consciousness, so they still have him in the ICU. But the nurses have been very good about letting us in to check on him, and they've even let Mrs. Carson sit in the room with him."

"How's she doing?"

Seth strolled over and stood at the other side of the cubicle. "She looks tired, but she said she's holding on. She wants to be there when he wakes up."

Alex shook his head. "She should be thinking *if* he wakes up."

"I've been thinking about her," Brad said. "I meant

to take Laura to see her, but we went to Melinda Stone's place instead. I think Laura might be able to help Mrs. Carson deal with this."

Alex nodded. "She might. After all, she counsels victims every day, and she sure knows what it's like to have someone you love die in a car bomb."

Seth pointed to the pictures on Brad's desk. "Have you come across anything else that might help in the investigation?"

"No, nothing yet." Brad sighed. "But I'll keep looking. Surely there's something in here that will lead us to Tony Lynch's successor." He glanced at his watch. "But I think I'll take a break and grab a bite of lunch first."

"We picked up something on the way back from the hospital, so we'll hold down the fort until you get back."

Brad nodded and pushed to his feet. He turned to leave but stopped when his cell phone rang. He pulled it from the clip on his belt and frowned at the unknown number.

He raised the phone to his ear. "Hello?"

"Detective Austin?"

Brad frowned at the unfamiliar voice. "Yes. Who's this?"

"This is Josh Nelson. I met you yesterday. I work with Laura at the clinic."

The reminder of the man with his arms around Laura rankled him, and his eyebrows arched. "I remember you, Mr. Nelson. What can I do for you?"

"Laura asked me to call you. She's in an ambulance on her way to the hospital and wanted you to know."

He gasped, and the breath was sucked out of his

body. He grabbed for the side of the desk to steady himself. "Ambulance? Why?"

Brad's knees grew weaker, and he groaned as he listened to Josh's account of Laura's car exploding. "It was awful, Detective Austin. There's nothing left of her car but a pile of burned-out metal."

"How badly was she hurt?" At the sound of Brad's loud voice Alex and Seth rushed across the room and waited beside him.

"I couldn't see any visible wounds, but Dr. Jones insisted she go to the hospital to make sure there were no internal problems."

"Was anybody else hurt?"

"There was a sanitation worker standing in the parking lot. He was hit by some metal and has a head wound. I don't know how serious it is. I don't think anybody else was injured. The police and firemen are here now."

Brad closed his eyes and rubbed his forehead. "Where is Laura?"

"The ambulance just left en route to the hospital."

"Thanks for calling. I'm on my way to the hospital now."

A few minutes later he was running down the hallway toward the exit. All he could think about was getting to Laura. He had thought he could protect her, but he hadn't been able to do it. Josh had said he thought she was okay, but he had to get to the hospital and see for himself. If anything happened to her, he would never forgive himself.

Fifteen minutes later, Brad cut the siren and flashing lights on his car as he pulled into the hospital parking lot. He was out the door and running toward the emergency room entrance almost before the engine had died.

The automatic doors slid open as he approached, and he dashed into the waiting area. As usual, nearly every seat in the room was filled with patients waiting their turn to see a doctor. He skidded to a stop at the receptionist's desk where a woman who appeared to be in her mid-fifties sat. A pencil protruded from her mass of gray hair. He pulled out his badge and shoved it close to her face. Her tired eyes flickered from it to his face.

"May I help you?" The words held no emotion. They might as well have been uttered by a robot.

"I'm Detective Austin with the Memphis Police Department. I'm here about Miss Laura Webber. She was transported here by ambulance from a car bombing."

The woman's expression didn't change. One would think car bombings were a routine part of her day. "If you'll have a seat, I'll check on her."

"You don't understand. I'm a policeman. I need to see her now."

She regarded him with a somber gaze. "I see badges every day, Detective, but not one of them gets by me until the doctor gives the okay. Now if you'll have a seat, I'll find out when you can talk to the patient."

Her no-nonsense attitude told him he had come up against someone who ruled her kingdom with an iron fist. At the moment, he needed to back off. He forced a smile to his face.

"I'd appreciate anything you can do to help me." He pointed to a couch across the room. "I'll be right over there."

She nodded. "I'm sure I'll be able to find you."

He turned and walked to the couch. He was about to sit down when a little girl who appeared to be about eight years old wandered from the water fountain, plopped down on one end of the sofa and opened a book. He looked around for an adult with her but saw no one.

He pointed to the couch. "Is your mother sitting here?"

Her big brown eyes stared up at him, and she shook her head. The barrettes clamped at the ends of tiny pigtails all over her head bounced up and down. "No, sir. My mama and me brought my grandma to the hospital to see the doctor. They told me to wait out here so I could read my new book. I like to read."

"And they left you out here all alone with all these people?"

"It's okay. Mrs. Johnson is watching me."

"And who is Mrs. Johnson?"

The child pointed to the receptionist Brad had talked with a few minutes ago. She stared at him with a steady gaze that reminded him of his fifth-grade teacher. He swallowed as he sank onto the couch next to the girl.

The child waved to Mrs. Johnson and then leaned over to whisper to him. "She makes sure I don't talk to strangers."

"But I'm a stranger, and you're talking to me."

She shook her head. "I saw you show your badge to Mrs. Johnson, so I knew you were a policeman. My mama says the police are our friends. So that means you're not a stranger."

Brad tried to suppress his smile, but he couldn't. "I see. And you say your grandmother is sick?"

"Uh-huh. But she's getting some medicine to help her feel better." She grinned, and the gaps where teeth had once been winked at him.

He glanced toward the receptionist's desk. Mrs. Johnson gave him another glance before she turned her attention to her computer.

"My name's Brad. What's yours?"

"I'm Tamika, and I'm gonna be in third grade when school starts." The door to the exam rooms opened, and a nurse pushed a wheelchair with an elderly man in it through the opening and down the hall that led into the hospital. When they moved out of sight, Tamika turned to him. "I'm gonna be a nurse when I grow up."

"I'm sure you'll be a very good one. My friend who's being treated right now is a nurse. She really likes it."

Her dark eyes crinkled at the corners, and she leaned closer. "Is your friend real sick?"

"I don't know. They haven't let me see her yet."

Tamika put her hand on his arm, and he looked down at the small fingers. Her chocolate-colored skin was a sharp contrast to the pale white of his. She patted his arm. "Have you prayed for her?"

To hear the words spoken so innocently by a child shocked him, and his mouth dropped open. "N-no. Why did you ask me that?"

She tilted her head to one side. "'Cause Mama says we need to pray for folks who are sick. I pray that my grandma will get better. Mama says that's all we can do now. Don't you want to pray for your friend?"

He shook his head and cleared his throat. "I can't do that. I don't know God very well."

She patted his arm again and smiled. "That's okay, mister. He knows you."

The words sliced into Brad's heart like a knife, and he almost doubled over in pain. Before he could say anything, a woman's voice sounded beside him. "Tamika, quit bothering the man. It's time to go home."

Brad looked up to see a woman with the same dark skin and eyes as the child next to him. He pushed to his feet. "She's not bothering me, ma'am. In fact, she's one of the smartest people I've talked to in a long time."

The mother chuckled. "She does like to talk. Takes after her daddy that way. But we have to go."

Tamika looked around, and then turned a questioning glance at her mother. "Where is Grandma?"

"She's going to stay overnight in the hospital. I'll take you home, then I'll come back and check on her."

"I hope she'll be okay," Brad said.

The woman's lips trembled. "I do, too. We just have to put it in God's hands."

Brad smiled down at Tamika and held out his hand. "It was good meeting you, Tamika. Tell your grandmother she sure is lucky to have such a smart granddaughter."

Tamika grinned and placed her hand in his. "I will." When he released her hand, she closed one eye, tilted her head to the side and looked up at him. "I forgot to ask what your friend's name is."

"It's Laura."

"Laura," she whispered. "I like that name. I'll pray for her tonight."

He swallowed hard. "Thank you. I'll tell her."

He watched as the mother and daughter walked over and spoke to Mrs. Johnson for a moment before they exited the building. Then he strode into the hallway that led back into the hospital. When he was out of sight of the patients in the waiting room, he leaned against the wall with his forehead touching the cool surface. He closed his eyes and tried to suppress the tears that threatened to spill down his cheeks.

His former pastor, his friends and his family had tried to talk to him for years about how he'd turned his back on God, but he wouldn't listen. Today a child he'd encountered in a hospital waiting room had spoken the words that had finally pierced the wall he'd put around his heart.

Tamika's words kept ringing in his head. *That's okay, mister. He knows you.*

The simple words reminded him that the Bible spoke of the kingdom of heaven being like a little child. In that moment Brad knew God had placed Tamika beside him in the waiting room to remind him that He wanted Brad to trust Him with the same unwavering faith that she had.

What he had told Tamika was exactly true. He had known God a long time ago, but he had pushed Him from his life. After Laura left, he'd been so angry with God for not helping him make her stay, that he had decided he could get along all right on his own.

All the time he knew that wasn't true. For six years he'd been lonely and sad. And all that time he'd been adamant that he was doing fine. Anyone who knew him, though, knew the truth. He had barely survived emotionally.

Then last night he'd been shocked when Jimmy Curtis said he and his wife prayed for him every day, and Laura had revealed that she prayed for him, too. Now a child reminded him of how important prayer had been to him when she told him that God knew him.

It was true. He might have left God, but God had never left him. He had provided him with friends who prayed for him, and He had guided Laura back.

"God, forgive me," he whispered.

For the first time in six years, he closed his eyes and prayed. He begged for forgiveness for turning his back on his God. Then he thanked God for those who'd never quit praying for him, and he prayed for healing for Laura.

Then last of all, he prayed that if it was God's will, that he and Laura would be able to overcome the hurt of the past and find their way back to each other.

He'd just whispered amen when he heard a sound nearby. He glanced over his shoulder, and Mrs. Johnson stood a few feet away. "Detective, you can go in to see Miss Webber now. She's in exam room ten."

He smiled at her and then glanced around the still crowded waiting room. "Thank you," he said. "And thank you for the job you do here in this busy emergency room. I know it's not easy."

Her eyes softened, and she nodded. "No, it's not, but it's where I serve. I try to do my best."

"I'm sure you do."

He walked past the woman and through the door that led to the exam rooms. Each cubicle he passed contained a patient, but the one he was most concerned with was in number ten. He couldn't wait to tell her what had happened to him.

* * *

Laura heard the footsteps coming down the hallway, and she knew it was Brad. It wasn't only the steady tap of his shoes on the floor, but it was his presence that she felt even before he stepped into the room. Her heart pricked at the thought of how badly she'd hurt him when she left with so little thought for his feelings. The only explanation she'd come up with was that she'd been young and still suffering from the trauma of her parents' deaths. She should have recognized the fact that Brad was the only person who had ever understood her, and she had chosen to turn her back on him.

When he hesitated outside the entrance to the exam room, she smiled. "It's okay, Brad. Come on in."

He eased in and walked over to the bed. His gaze raked over her as if he was trying to see any visible signs of injury. After a moment he smiled. "Josh said you weren't injured, but I was afraid to believe him."

"I'm all right." She pointed to a chair next to the bed. "Thank you for coming. I wanted you to know."

He sat down and pulled the chair closer to her bed. "I wouldn't be anywhere else. Have you called Charles and Nora?"

"I had the nurse call them after I got here. She said they were on their way."

Her arm lay out from under the covers, and he reached over and curled his fingers around hers. "I'm so sorry I let this happen to you, Laura."

She frowned and shook her head. "You didn't let this happen, Brad. These people have been after me ever since I did that interview. You have tried every way to help me, and I appreciate it more than you'll ever know."

He grasped her hand tighter and rubbed the back of her hand with his thumb. "I should have insisted you stay away from work. And I shouldn't have let you out of my sight. It's my fault you're in here."

She covered his hand with her free one and smiled. "It's not your fault. It's those monsters who killed my parents and now would like to do the same to me. But we'll get them. I know we will."

His eyes widened in surprise. "You're not going to be involved in this investigation any more. I'm not going to have your death on my conscience."

She smiled. "Brad, do you think you can order me to give this up?" She shook her head. "Not at this point. They must be scared we're getting close, or they wouldn't have tried to kill me in broad daylight in view of lots of people."

He sighed and arched his eyebrows. "We'll talk about this later. Right now we need to concentrate on getting you well."

"I'm fine. The doctor says there are no internal injuries, and I can go home when Charles and Nora get here. I want you to go back to work and not worry about me."

His hand tightened on hers. "I'll go back to work, but I doubt if I can quit worrying. Is it okay if I come by tonight to see you?"

She blinked back the tears that she could feel forming and smiled. "I would like that very much."

"Good. I'll stay with you until Charles and Nora get here. I need to tell you what happened to me in the waiting room."

For the next few minutes he told her about his meeting with the little girl whose words had caused him to examine his life for the first time in years. He told her how he'd asked God to forgive him for ignoring Him all those years and thanked Him for friends like Jimmy and her, and for his family who'd continued to pray for him when he wasn't a lovable person.

When he finished, she wiped at a tear that rolled from her eye. "Oh, Brad. I'm so happy for you. I've learned how important it is to have faith to fall back on when things aren't going well in your life. I only hope this means you've finally forgiven me for hurting you."

His dark eyes stared at her, and her heartbeat quickened. After a moment he smiled, leaned forward and kissed her on the forehead. "I have forgiven you, Laura, but I know I'm at fault, too, in what happened between us. I hope you've forgiven me."

"I have." She took a deep breath. "Where do we go from here?"

"I think we need to get to know each other again. Then maybe when this case is closed, we can talk about that."

She smiled. "That sounds good to me."

Whatever he was about to say was interrupted by a high-pitched voice in the hallway. "Where is Laura Webber? I need to see her right away."

Laura looked up at Brad and smiled. "It sounds like Nora's here."

Brad barely had time to step out of the way as Nora barreled into the room and toward the bed. Charles followed behind her. Nora grabbed Laura's hand. "Are you all right?"

"Yes, Nora. I'm fine. Not one scratch."

Nora whirled to face Brad. "How could this happen at her workplace?"

"I don't know. I'm sure the lab will let us know what kind of bomb was involved. Since she didn't start the car, it wasn't connected to the engine. My guess would be it was on a timer or it was detonated from a remote location."

Charles's eyes grew large. "If it was detonated, wouldn't somebody have to be nearby?"

"Possibly."

Charles frowned and shook his head. "I didn't feel good about you going back to work, and this proves that I was right. You're not to leave the house from now on unless you are with Brad or me. Do you understand?"

Laura looked from Brad, who nodded his agreement, and back to Charles. "Okay, you win." Nora grasped her hand, and Charles wrapped his fingers around the other one. Laura closed her eyes and thanked God for placing Charles and Nora in her life. With Mark in North Carolina and her uncle and aunt in California, they were the only family she had.

She opened her eyes and glanced at Brad. The way he was looking at her made her skin grow warm. If things worked out like she hoped, maybe she'd soon have Brad back in her life, too. She certainly hoped so.

TWELVE

Laura wiped a tear from her cheek as the movie credits began to roll down the television screen. She glanced at Brad who sat beside her on the sofa and frowned at the amused expression on his face. "You know I've always loved that movie."

He reached for the remote and pushed the mute button. "I should have known better than to let you talk me into watching that one again. I must have watched it a hundred times with you when we were in high school."

She swatted him on the arm and frowned. "You're exaggerating. If you had your way, it would only be action or horror."

His eyebrows arched. "That's better than sitting through a chick flick over and over."

"Don't complain to me. You slept through most of it."

He picked up the empty popcorn bowl that sat on the couch between them. "Yeah, and you ate all the popcorn."

"Which goes to prove if you snooze, you lose." She made a face at him and grabbed the bowl out of his hands. "I'll take this back to the kitchen."

Before she could move, he grabbed her arm. "Don't

go." The touch of his hand sent a tingle of pleasure up her arm, and she looked at him. He narrowed his eyes and pulled her closer. "I wasn't sleeping, Laura. I was thinking how glad I was to be here with you tonight. It felt right for us to be together again."

"I know," she whispered.

He swallowed, and his Adam's apple bobbed. "I've missed you so much. I tried to tell myself I didn't, but I knew I did."

Tears filled her eyes. "I've missed you, too, Brad."

He shook his head. "Then why did you get engaged so soon after going to Raleigh?"

"I don't know. Chet was a good man, and he opened my eyes to how much I needed God in my life. I thought I'd be happy with him, but I was only kidding myself. And you had other women in your life after me."

"I did, but none of them were you." He paused as if he was debating whether or not to say what else was on his mind. She waited for him to decide. "There's something I need to know."

"What?"

"Why didn't you contact me when you moved back to Memphis? How could you live in the same city as me for a year and not let me know?"

Tears filled her eyes. "I wanted to call you. In fact, I thought about it all the time. But Grace told me you'd broken up with the woman you'd been seeing, and I didn't want to be a reminder of two broken relationships. Besides, I thought you despised me, and I didn't think I could stand to see hatred for me in your eyes. But that all changed the night I was abducted. I didn't want anybody but you."

He chuckled. "I've never been as surprised in my life as I was when I found you asleep at my desk. I told myself I should turn your case over to Alex or Seth, but I couldn't stay away from you. My feelings about you were so mixed up. One minute I was angry with you and the next I was so glad you were back."

"I'm not the girl I was when I left here, Brad."

"No, you're not, but I'm not the same, either. Sometimes I think about those two young kids, and I wish I could give them some advice. But I doubt if they'd listen."

She reached out and caressed his cheek. "Maybe they would now that they're grown and realize even when you're in love, it takes a lot of compromise and understanding to make a relationship work."

He placed his hand on hers, brought her fingers to his lips and kissed them. "I hope so." After a moment he released her hand and sighed. "I think that's enough rekindling of old memories for tonight. I'd better be going. I'll come by to see you tomorrow."

"Okay." As they walked to the front door, Laura debated how she could ask him what she'd wanted to all night. Finally she decided the only way was to come out and say it. "About tomorrow…"

He had just grabbed the doorknob when he paused and turned toward her. "What about tomorrow?"

"I know you want me to stay in, and I know you're only thinking of my welfare. But there's something I need to do tomorrow."

His eyes narrowed. "What is it?"

"Tomorrow afternoon I have the last counseling session with a group I've been working with for a year. I need to meet with them at the hospital."

He raked his hand through his hair. "Laura, think of what happened today. I don't want another…"

"I don't, either. I'll do the session and come right back here. I asked Charles if he could go with me, but he's tied up with business all day. Is there any way I could get a police officer to accompany me?"

He stared at her a moment, propped his hands on his hips and exhaled. "You are one stubborn woman. You almost get killed not once, not twice, but three times and you still insist on putting yourself in danger."

"I can't let them win, Brad. I have to let them know that they're not going to stop me. Those people in my class tomorrow have had some horrible things happen in their lives. We've been working together for a year, but I don't know if they'll ever be able to face their memories. I feel I need to be there for them."

He held up his hands in surrender. "Okay, I give up. I need to go check on Nathan Carson at the hospital tomorrow afternoon, so I'll go with you to class."

"Then could I go with you to see the Carsons? You know you said you'd take me."

He nodded. "I did say that. What time is your session?"

"Two o'clock."

"I'll pick you up at one and stay with you during your class. Then we'll go see the Carsons, and I'll bring you back to Charles and Nora's house. How's that?"

She reached up and kissed him on the cheek. "Thank you. I appreciate it."

When she pulled back, he blinked in surprise and touched his face where she'd kissed him. "Good night, Laura."

"Good night, Brad."

She closed the door behind him and waited until she heard his car pull away from the house before she headed to the stairway. Before she could mount the first riser, she looked up to see Nora coming downstairs. "I thought you and Charles had gone to bed."

Nora stopped beside her and yawned. "Charles is sound asleep, but I can't drop off. I thought maybe a cup of cocoa would help. Want to join me?"

"No, thanks. It's been a trying day. I think I'll go to bed."

Nora pulled her robe tighter around her and shivered. "It was a terrifying day." Nora took a deep breath. "But on a happier note, you and Brad seem to be getting along well. I really hope it works out for you."

"Thanks. Maybe when all these threats against me have been resolved, we can work on a relationship. Right now there's too much going on."

"I suppose you're right. Did you talk to Brad about going to the hospital tomorrow?"

"Yes. He wasn't too happy about it at first, but he's going with me. After my class he wants to take me to meet the wife of the man who was in the other car bombing."

Nora nodded. "How's he doing?"

"About the same I think. He hasn't regained consciousness. I thought I might be able to help his wife since I've lived through the same thing she's experiencing right now."

"I'm sure you can." Nora yawned. "Now I think I'll get that cocoa. Are you sure you don't want any?"

"No, thanks. I'm off to bed. Good night."

As Laura climbed the stairs, she thought of the evening she and Brad had spent together. They hadn't talked much during the movie, but the silence had been a comfortable one. Their short conversation afterward had given her hope that maybe they could find their way back to each other.

But before she could give that any serious thought, she had to find out who wanted to kill her.

The next afternoon, Brad waited in the hospital hallway and watched Laura shake hands with each of her clients as they left her office. The last to leave was a young woman who appeared to be in her mid-thirties. Laura leaned closer and listened as the woman spoke in hushed tones. Although her eyes held a sad look, a feeble smile pulled at her lips.

"Thank you, Laura, for everything you've done for me this past year. I will never forget what's happened, but you've given me the strength to face whatever the future holds," the young woman said.

Laura smiled and squeezed the woman's hand tighter. "It's not going to be easy, Jane, but you have the tools that are going to help you cope on the bad days. And remember, I'll be praying for you. If you ever need me, you know how to get in touch."

"I do."

As Jane walked down the hallway, Laura's gaze followed her. Then she sighed and glanced at him. "I need to put up the folding chairs before we go to Mr. Carson's room. Want to help?"

He grinned. "Sure. I'll take care of the chairs while you finish up anything else you have to do."

"Thanks."

He took a step toward her office but stopped when his cell phone rang. He pulled it from the clip and glanced down to see Rick Thompson's name on caller ID. "I need to take this."

"Go ahead. I'll finish up in my office while you're talking."

He nodded and raised the phone to his ear. "Hello."

"Austin, it's Rick. I'm sorry I haven't gotten back to you before this, but so far there's been nothing to report."

Brad walked into the hall, leaned against the wall and rubbed his hand across his forehead. "You haven't found a link between Lucas Pennington and Tony Lynch?"

"No, but Lynch knew how to hide things. I've run down dozens of rabbit trails trying to find something, but so far I haven't found anything that ties Pennington to him."

Brad's shoulders slumped, and he sighed. "I appreciate you trying anyway."

"Hey, I'm not giving up. I wanted to check in and let you know how things have gone so far. But I may have stumbled on something a few minutes ago."

For the first time in days Brad felt a burst of hope, and he straightened to his full height. "What is it?"

"It's hard to know if it's going to lead to anything. But I found this corporation that Lynch had set up. When I got into it more, I found it was a dummy corporation. I'm in the process now of trying to find the real businesses he's trying to hide. So far it's been a maze of blind alleys, but I'm not giving up. Whoever set this thing up for him is good."

"You mean 'whoever' like in a lawyer such as Lucas Pennington?"

"You got it. Somebody knew what they were doing,

und Pennington does a lot of corporate law. I'm going to find these companies and their hidden boards of directors. When I do, I should have an answer for you."

"Keep digging, Rick, and let me know as soon as you find something."

"Will do."

Brad slipped his phone back in the clip on his belt just as Laura walked out of her office and closed the door behind her. "I took care of everything inside. I don't mean to be paranoid, but did your phone call have anything to do with me?"

"As a matter of fact it did. Rick Thompson is doing some more computer searches for me, but he doesn't have anything yet. He'll call when he does. I'll go put away the chairs now."

"Nope, I've already done that. I suppose we're ready to go see the Carsons."

"I guess so." He pointed down the hallway toward the elevators. "After you."

As they walked toward the elevator, he reached out to touch the small of her back. This time he didn't draw back like he had at Ribs and More. He smiled at how right this felt. He'd always heard that old habits are hard to break, and he kept discovering the truth in that statement.

When he and Laura were younger, they'd spent every spare minute together. Now that she was back, he was discovering that being with her was one habit he hoped he never broke. He could only pray she felt the same way.

When she saw the FBI agent outside Nathan Carson's room, it reminded her that she and the patient inside shared something few people did. They had both been targeted by people who had no regard for human life. She said a quick prayer of thanks that the attempts on her life had been unsuccessful and that Nathan might live.

When she and Brad walked past the agent, the bond she'd felt in the hallway for the Carson family grew stronger. She eased into the dimly lit room and stared at the still figure in the bed. It was difficult to tell much about his features with his head swathed in bandages and wires hooked to his body. As a nurse, she knew right away the seriousness of his condition.

His wife rose from a chair at his bedside when they entered and smiled when she saw Brad. "Detective Austin, it's good to see you again. Your partners have been here every day, and they have been so kind."

Brad took her hand in both of his and nodded. "I'm glad they have. I've been working on another case, or I would have been here earlier." He touched Laura's elbow and drew her closer. "This is Laura Webber. She has a lot in common with you and your family."

Mrs. Carson's eyebrows arched. "Oh? How's that?"

As Laura told of the incident that had devastated her family nearly twenty years ago, Mrs. Carson's eyes grew sad. She glanced at her husband from time to time as Laura spoke and brushed at her tears several times.

Laura concluded her story and grasped Mrs. Carson's hand. "Sometimes people say they know how a person feels, but they really don't if they haven't experienced what that person is going through at the time. I do know how you feel. I've lived with it since I was ten years old. I only hope your nightmare doesn't end like mine did."

Mrs. Carson squeezed Laura's hand, then reached up and hugged her. "I'm so sorry."

"Thank you. And I want you to know I will be glad to help you any way I can. I'm a forensic nurse at Cornerstone Clinic. I counsel patients whose family members have been victims of violent crime. I do sessions at the clinic and at the hospital. If you or your daughter need any help, I'm available." Laura pulled her card out and handed it to her.

Mrs. Carson stared at the card a moment before she looked up at Laura. "What have you found in your life to be the most important thing that's helped you deal with your parents' deaths?"

"I only found the most important thing a few years ago, and it's made all the difference in the world. When I turned my life over to God, He filled me with the strength to face every day. So for me it's been having faith in God."

She smiled. "I'm glad to hear you say that. Right now my faith and my prayers are the only thing getting me through this time. I think it would do my daughter and me a lot of good to attend some of your sessions."

"I'd be happy to have you. My cell phone number is on that card. Call me anytime, and I'll get you set up."

"Thank you."

Brad cleared his throat, and they both glanced at him. "Mrs. Carson," he said, "I think Laura could help you, too. Our office wants to catch the people who did this. We believe the people who killed Laura's parents are responsible for what happened to your husband, too. We're doing everything we can to find them. People are working as we speak on a lead that I believe will lead us to the head of the crime organization."

"Oh, that's good news," she answered.

Brad pointed to the chair where she'd been sitting. "I have a few questions I'd like to run by you if you don't mind. Why don't you sit back down while we talk?"

Brad waited until Mrs. Carson was seated before he scooted a chair in front of her and took a seat. Just as Brad started to ask his first question, the alarm on the IV bag began to beep. Mrs. Carson propped her hands on the arms of her chair to push to her feet, but Laura shook her head.

"It's okay. I think one of the lines has gotten twisted. I'll get the nurse to check it out."

Mrs. Carson sighed with relief and sank back into the chair as Laura headed to the door. Brad glanced over his shoulder. "Laura, where are you going?"

"To the nurses' station to make sure they heard the alarm. I'll be right back."

"Okay." He turned back to Mrs. Carson as she exited the room and walked past the agent outside.

Laura spotted a nurse at the end of the hall and waved to her. "We've got an IV problem in here."

She hurried toward Laura and stopped before she entered the room. "I was on my way, but a patient yelled at me from another room."

Laura chuckled. "I'm a nurse, too. I know how hectic it can get."

The nurse pushed the door open and entered the room. Laura took a step to follow her but stopped when her cell phone rang. She pulled it from her pocket and looked in surprise at the name displayed on the caller ID.

She turned her back on the agent and walked back down the hallway. "Josh? I wasn't expecting a call from you."

"I know. I thought you'd be at work today, but Dr. Jones said you were only doing your counseling session at the hospital this afternoon. I'm at your office now, but you're not here. Have you already left?"

"No, I'm visiting a patient. Why did you come to my office?"

"I wanted to say goodbye before I left town."

Her hand tightened on the phone. "You're leaving Memphis? Will you be back?"

He sighed. "I don't know. Things aren't going well with my dad, and I need to go home and help my mom. You're really the only friend I made at work, and I wanted to say goodbye in person before I left."

Laura glanced back down the hall at the FBI agent. His back was turned to her as he chatted with a young nurses' aide outside Nathan's room. "You're at my office now?"

"Yeah, I'm right in front of the door."

"Then I'll run back down there to tell you goodbye."

"I'd like that, Laura."

She disconnected the call, stuck the phone back in her pants pocket and hurried over to the elevator. The door opened as soon as she punched the button. As the elevator descended to the first floor where her office was located, she regretted her rash decision. Brad had made it clear that he didn't want her going off alone. She would make her conversation with Josh short, and she would hurry back upstairs.

When she reached her office, Josh was leaning against the wall in the same spot Brad had been when she walked out of her class earlier. He straightened and smiled as she walked toward him. His gaze drifted over her shoulder and then came back to rest on her.

"I thought you might have Detective Austin with you."

"No, he's still upstairs."

He took a deep breath. "Thanks for coming down. I really wanted to see you before I left. If I don't get back, I hope we can stay in touch."

"You know where I'll be. Call me anytime."

"I will." He stuck his hands in his pockets and stared down at the floor. "It's no secret that I was attracted to you from the very first. I'm sorry it didn't work out."

She smiled. "I don't think we're right for each other, Josh. It was better for us to be friends."

His gaze raked her face, and he nodded. "So, how about giving a friend a hug before he takes off on the long ride home?"

She hesitated a moment before she smiled. "All right."

His left arm circled her waist and drew her close as Laura closed her eyes and wrapped her arms around his neck. Her eyes popped open in surprise the moment the circular barrel pressed into her stomach.

She pulled her arms loose and propped her hands against his shoulders. She struggled to escape his grip, but he tightened his hold on her.

"Don't fight me, Laura. This gun has a silencer on it. I'll kill you right here where you stand."

Her body trembled, but she quit struggling against him. "Wh-what do you want?"

"I want you to come with me." He pulled her to his side where he held her with his left hand and pushed the gun into her ribs with the other. "If you make one sound as we leave this hospital, it will be your last. Do you understand?"

She nodded and shuffled forward when he began to walk. The halls were deserted as they moved to the exit. She glanced up at a security camera as they passed, and her heart plummeted to the pit of her stomach when she remembered the memo she'd received last week. The system overhaul had been scheduled for today, and none of the cameras were working.

They exited the building, and Josh pulled her toward a black SUV that sat idling outside. He opened the door, pushed her inside and crawled in behind her. "Drive," he said to a faceless driver, and the vehicle pulled away.

Laura glanced out the window as the hospital receded from sight and groaned. No one had seen her leave, and there was no recording of Josh forcing her outside.

Fear like she'd never known rushed up inside her and threatened to choke her. Brad had always said she was stubborn, and he was right. She'd ignored his warnings and had gone off by herself without telling him. Now she would have to suffer the consequences of that choice, and she feared it might be the last one she would ever face.

THIRTEEN

Laura huddled in the corner of the seat and stared at Josh beside her, his gun pointed in her direction. She still couldn't believe what was happening. Josh had always been the perfect gentleman at work. She would never have suspected him of being able to kill anybody, but the determined look on his face now told her she'd been wrong.

"Why, Josh? Why are you doing this to me?"

He turned an icy stare to her. "It's called survival, Laura. If you're scared enough, you'll do whatever it takes to stay alive."

"Tell me who you're scared of. I'll go with you to Brad, and he'll take care of it."

He threw back his head and laughed. "I think it's a little too late for that. Maybe if I'd done that at first, things would be different. But I didn't, and there's no turning back now."

She frowned. "I don't understand. Who are you afraid of?"

"It doesn't matter anymore. After I deliver you to them, my debt will be paid, and I'm out of Memphis for good."

She leaned toward him and gritted her teeth. "It

matters to me who wants to kill me. They murdered my parents, and now they want me dead. I think I have a right to know how a person with a promising future could get involved with a gang of murderers."

He frowned and closed his eyes for a moment. "I was stupid, Laura. When I got that job at Cornerstone, I was thrilled to death. One night I ended up with a bunch of my friends down on Beale Street, and one of them knew where there was a private poker game going on. I went along to watch, but I ended up playing. After that, I went back again and again until I was hooked and so far in the hole I knew I'd never be able to pay off my gambling debt."

"That's when you should have gone to the police. Gambling is illegal in this state. If you had cooperated with them, they would have helped you."

"Well, I didn't go. Then the guy I owed money to starting pressuring me to pay up. I knew I couldn't, and they gave me an option. I could spy on you at work, and they'd forgive my debt. I thought it wouldn't hurt anything just to pass along information, but they started to want more and more. The night I helped abduct you, I told them I couldn't do it anymore."

She bolted up straight in her seat, her eyes wide. "You were with them when they took me down to the river?"

He bit down on his lip and groaned. "Yeah, I was driving." He exhaled a deep breath before he continued. "Anyway, after I threatened to quit, they burned my parents' house down and said they'd go back and kill them if I didn't keep working for them." He shrugged. "So here we are. End of story."

The memory of her car exploding flashed in her

mind, and she gasped. "Did you have anything to do with blowing up my car?"

His mouth hardened into a straight line, and he looked out the car window for a few seconds before he answered. "Yeah. I pushed the remote. You were supposed to die that day."

Brad had said it probably was a timer or a remote, but she would never have suspected one of her coworkers of trying to kill her. "If I was supposed to die, what happened?"

He shook his head, and he raked his hand through his hair. "I messed up, that's what happened. I was inside the building, and I couldn't see your car in the parking lot. I knew when you went out the door. And then I heard a car door slam and a car engine start, and I thought it was you. I pushed the button, but it wasn't your car."

"No, it was Lucy. She left before me."

He gave a nervous laugh. "Yeah, so I found out. They've given me one more chance to make good, or they're going back after my parents. I can't mess up this time."

Laura searched her heart for the contempt she knew she should feel for Josh, but it wasn't there. Instead she felt a great sadness that he had been caught up in a web of evil that had existed for years. Her heart pricked at the thought of his parents and what they had suffered because of their son's mistakes.

"I'm sorry, Josh."

He frowned. "Sorry for what?"

"For you, and for your parents. You've let evil touch the people you're supposed to love the most in your life. I hope they never find out what you've done."

His stony features cracked, and she thought she saw tears in his eyes. Then it vanished, and he snarled as he straightened in the seat. "Well, there's one sure thing. *You're* not going to tell them about me."

His words sent chill bumps racing up her spine. She wrapped her arms around her waist, hugged herself and glanced out the car window. She caught sight of a street sign and recognized it as one in the northern part of the city. She'd never been in this area much and had no idea where they might be going.

Brad's face flashed in her mind, and she wondered if he was already looking for her. If he was, she had no idea how he would ever find her. Nothing had been left behind that would give him a clue to her whereabouts, and as best she could tell no one had seen them leave the hospital.

At this point, all she could do was pray that he would find her before it was too late.

Brad closed the notebook in which he'd been jotting down Mrs. Carson's answers as he had talked with her and glanced over his shoulder. With a start he realized for the first time that Laura wasn't in the room. He'd thought she came back in when the nurse had checked Nathan's IV line, but she wasn't here now.

He jumped to his feet and scanned the room again. "Where's Laura?"

Mrs. Carson pushed to her feet and frowned. "I don't know. She never came back after she went for the nurse."

Brad whirled to face her. "She's been gone all this time?"

A puzzled look flashed across Mrs. Carson's face,

and she nodded. "Is something wrong? I thought since she was a nurse she probably had stayed down the hall to talk to the nurses."

Brad raked his hand through his hair. "She's not supposed to be out of my sight. She's had several attempts on her life this week."

Mrs. Carson's eyes grew wide, and she put her hand in front of her mouth. "If I'd known that, I would have told you she didn't come back. I'm sorry."

He shook his head. "It's not your fault. I've got to find her."

He ran to the door and jerked it open. The agent looked up from the chair where he sat outside the door and jumped to his feet when Brad dashed into the hall. "Is something wrong?"

Brad looked up and down the hall before he turned back to him. "The girl that was with me came out to get a nurse a little while ago. Did you see where she went?"

He shook his head. "I saw her come out, but I don't know where she went after that."

The nurse who had adjusted the IV line stepped into the hall from a patient's room two doors down from Nathan's, and Brad ran to her. "Do you remember the young woman who came to tell you the alarm was going off on the IV in Mr. Carson's room?"

"Yes." She glanced at the door to Nathan's room. "Is it beeping again?"

"No, I need to know if you saw where the young woman went."

"The one who said she is a nurse?"

"Yes, that's the one."

"She didn't follow me into the room. I looked back at her, and she was talking on her cell phone."

"Her cell phone?" He turned to the agent who'd followed him down the hall. "Did you see her on her cell phone?"

He nodded. "Yeah, come to think of it, I did. It rang just as she started back into the room."

"Do you know who was calling?"

His forehead wrinkled as if he was in deep thought, and then he shook his head. "I didn't hear her say a name."

Brad turned back to the nurse. "How do I contact security about checking the surveillance cameras in the halls? Maybe I can see where she went."

She shook her head. "I'm sorry, sir. That wouldn't do any good. All the cameras are down today because of a scheduled overhaul."

Fear stabbed Brad in the stomach, and he turned and ran toward the elevators. Laura knew better than to leave without telling him. Something must have happened. He pushed the button for the elevator, but when the doors didn't open right away, he dashed to the exit sign at the end of the hallway and rushed down the stairs.

Minutes later he arrived on the first floor, but he didn't stop until he reached Laura's office. His hopes collapsed when he turned the knob, but it wouldn't open.

"That office is locked." He whirled to see a custodian with a rolling trash cart stopped a few feet away.

Brad pulled out his badge and held it up. "I'm looking for Laura Webber. This is her office. Have you seen her in the past few minutes?"

The man pushed the cap he wore back on his head and nodded. "I saw her leaving."

"Leaving?" Brad's mouth dropped open, and he took a step toward the man.

"Yeah. I was out at the Dumpster with a load of trash when I saw her come out the door to a car in the parking lot. She was with this fellow who had her all hugged up to him. I figured it was her boyfriend."

"Had you ever seen him before?"

He shook his head. "I just saw his back. Couldn't tell you what he looked like."

"What kind of car did they get in?"

The man stroked his chin. "Well, it was big, and it was black. I think they call them SUVs, but I don't know what make it was. I'm not too familiar with cars like that."

"Thanks," Brad called over his shoulder as he bolted down the hall and into the parking lot. He pulled his cell phone from his pocket as he ran and punched in Bill Diamond's number.

He answered right away. "Diamond."

"Bill, this is Brad Austin. This is an emergency, and I need the FBI's help right away."

"What is it, Brad?"

"Laura Webber, the daughter of Lawrence Webber, has been kidnapped. It has to be Tony Lynch's people. I have no idea where they've taken her, but I thought we might be able to trace her cell phone. Can you get the cell phone provider to track the towers her phone is hitting and also to see who her last calls were from?"

"I can. Where are you now?"

"At the hospital."

"Then get to my office. I'll be on it by the time you get here."

Brad jumped in his car and roared out of the parking

lot. He was relieved to see that traffic was lighter than usual, and he weaved in and out of it with his lights flashing and siren wailing. Ten minutes later he pulled into the parking lot for the Memphis FBI field office.

When he burst into Bill's office, Bill was just hanging up his desk phone. "You got here in record time."

"There wasn't much traffic. Have you started tracking the phone yet?"

Bill nodded. "An agent is at the phone company now. We should be hearing something soon. Right now, all we can do is wait."

Brad raked his hand through his hair and began to pace back and forth. "I can't stand to think that they may have already killed her or have hurt her in some way."

Bill looked at him in surprise. "You sound like this is something personal. Is this young woman more than a victim to you?"

"Yes, she is, and I want to be able to tell her she is. If something happens to her, I'll never forgive myself for letting her out of my sight."

Bill walked over to him and put his hand on Brad's shoulder. "You need to get your emotions under control. If you want to help her, you need to quit thinking like a man in love and start thinking like a policeman, the way you're trained to do."

Brad nodded. "You're right. I need to concentrate on saving her."

"I'll get you a cup of coffee while we're waiting for the phone records."

Brad sank down in a chair and thought of the things he and Laura had said to each other last night. The things she'd said led him to believe she was ready for the two of them to work on their relationship. He wanted that more than he'd ever wanted anything. Laura had been a part of him since he was fourteen years old, and he wanted her back in his life. He only hoped he got the chance to ask her.

The SUV pulled off the paved street and drove down a deserted gravel road. Laura had caught a glimpse of the Mississippi River before they left the main highway, but now tall trees blocked her view. A small opening in the trees gave her the first clue of their destination when she spotted the mainmast of some kind of ship stretching into the sky.

Her stomach clenched in fear at the thought that flashed in her mind. Brad had said the undercover policeman who'd been killed had stumbled on some information about human trafficking. Was that to be her fate? Sent on a ship to some unknown destination and be subjected to a lifestyle that turned her stomach?

As they rounded a curve in the road, Laura caught sight of a barge dock at the edge of the river. The vessel with the tall mainmast, a tugboat with six flat-bottomed barges lashed together in front of it, floated on the water. Two of the barges held large containers stacked on top of each other. They reminded her of the trailers on the eighteen-wheeler trucks she'd seen on the interstate the day she and Brad went to Nashville.

Brad. Just the thought of his name brought tears to her eyes. What was he doing right now? Was he looking for her, or did he realize like she did that her situation was hopeless? She didn't know how he would be able to find her in this deserted place.

"It's time to get out." Josh's voice brought her back to the present, and she swiveled in her seat to face him.

"It's not too late, Josh. You can still let me go, and I'll tell the police you helped save me."

He shook his head. "I wish it was that easy, Laura. But these people are everywhere. If I don't go through with this, they'll kill my parents. I can't let that happen."

He opened the car door, grabbed her by the arm and yanked her across the seat. She slid out the door and grabbed for something to hold on to as she lost her balance and hit the ground with a thud. Josh reached down and jerked her to her feet.

The driver of the car emerged and glared at Josh. "Can you handle her by yourself, or do you need help?"

Josh shook his head and tightened his grip on her. "I've got this."

Laura, half stumbling and half walking, struggled to keep up with Josh as he strode toward the riverbank and then down the dock. When they reached the boarding area of the tugboat, he forced her to climb from the dock into the boat.

Two men waited for them on board and nodded their approval to Josh when he pushed her forward to stand in front of them. "So, Miss Webber, we meet again."

She jerked her head up at the familiar voice she'd first heard the night she'd been abducted. She clenched her fists at her sides and gritted her teeth. "You should have called and let me know I was to be your guest."

A sinister laugh rumbled in his throat. "Sarcasm will get you nowhere with me. But you needn't worry. I don't intend on your being my guest for very long."

Fear knotted her stomach, and her legs shook. "Are you going to tell me what you have planned for me?"

"Not just yet. Anticipation is always so much more fun, don't you think?" He directed a stern look in Josh's direction. "Did you search her before you brought her aboard?"

"No. She didn't have anything with her."

The man rolled his eyes and sighed. "That's what I'd expect from an amateur." He pointed to her pocket. "Didn't you notice the bulge in her pocket? She has something in there." He held out his hand. "Give it to me, Miss Webber."

Laura stuck her hand in her pocket, pulled out her phone and handed it to the man who held it up for Josh to see. "We can't have her calling the cops while she's our guest, can we?"

Josh's face turned red, and he shook his head. "N-no. I'm sorry. I didn't think."

"That's becoming a habit with you," the man growled before he drew back and hurled her phone into the river. It splashed, and then sank out of sight.

Laura had only a moment to grieve over her last connection to the outside world before one of the large containers on the barge opened, and a man climbed out. Her eyes grew wide as he jumped to the deck below and made his way toward where they stood on the tugboat.

When he reached them, he addressed the man who had abducted her. "They haven't eaten in over twenty-four hours. Do you want me to give them anything?"

The man shook his head. "No. They can eat when they get to where they're going."

"What about water? It's mighty hot in there."

"We don't have time to coddle them We're going to cast off before long. You can give them some water tonight when we're under way."

The man shrugged. "You're the boss." He turned and headed back to the still-open container.

Laura cringed at the muffled sobs and groans drifting from the cargo container. She couldn't believe what she was witnessing. There were people inside that trailer, and they were suffering. The barge was being used to transport human beings upriver.

"You're human traffickers," she cried. "Where are you taking those people?"

The man who'd abducted her took a threatening step toward her. "That's none of your business," he snarled.

"But that's despicable. Only the vilest creatures would do something like that to another person. What's going to happen to them?"

"Vile, huh?" He cocked one eyebrow and smiled. "Do you really want to know what we're going to do with them?"

"Yes."

He shrugged. "All right. The men will be sold to big farms across the country, and the women will end up in brothels. Is that what you wanted to know?"

She sucked in her breath. "Am I going to share the same fate?"

He laughed, put his finger under her chin and lifted her face. "Not you, sweetheart. We have something else in store for you."

She jerked her head away from his touch. "Get your hands off me."

Her head snapped back from the force of his slap, and he circled her neck with his fingers. He squeezed until the breath almost left her body. "I tried to warn you," he said. "But you just wouldn't listen. Now you're going to pay."

He released his hold and gave her a shove. She stumbled backward into Josh's arms. He propped her back on her feet and cleared his throat. "Look, I need to get out of here. I've done everything you've asked. Now we should be square. My debts are paid, and I want my parents left alone."

The man nodded. "We're almost finished. There's just one more thing."

Josh frowned. "What?"

"This." The gunshot sounded almost before he had finished speaking.

Laura glanced in shock at the gun that had appeared in the man's hand and then to Josh who was clutching his stomach. He stared down in surprise at the blood trickling between his clutched fingers and then slumped to the deck.

"Josh!" Laura dropped to her knees beside him, but strong fingers wrapped around her arm and yanked her to her feet.

"Leave him alone."

"But he's hurt." She struggled against her captor, but she couldn't get loose.

"No, he's dead," the man said and pulled her away. He turned to the other person with him. "Tie her up and put her in wheelhouse. We'll let the boss decide what he wants to do with her when he gets here. Then get back down here and stow this body. We'll drop him overboard somewhere upriver tonight."

The other man grabbed her arm and stuck a gun in her side. "We're going to climb the bridge ladder to the wheelhouse. If you make one false move, I'll kill you. Understand?"

She nodded. "Yes."

Laura walked to the bow of the boat and began her climb up the bridge ladder. Her knees wobbled, and she clutched at the handrails to support herself as she inched upward. When she finally reached the deck around the wheelhouse, the man pushed her inside toward a coiled length of rope in one corner where he bound her hands and feet securely. Then without a word to her, he rose and left her there. She heard his footsteps as he descended the ladder to the deck below.

Minutes passed, and no one came. She wondered where the men had gone, what they had done with Josh's body, and how badly the people locked in the container were suffering. But most of her thoughts were of Brad and where he was at the moment.

Big tears formed in her eyes and rolled down her cheeks. Last night her hopes had been so high that she and Brad would be able to reunite and have a future together. Now the prospects for that looked bleak. She wondered if she was destined to end up at the bottom of the Mississippi River along with Josh. She leaned her head against the wall and prayed that God would somehow help Brad discover a way to find her.

She had just finished her prayer when she heard the roar of a boat motor coming toward the tug. She listened as it slowed and came to a stop. Shuffling noises from below told her that other people had boarded the boat. Were they here to see her?

As if in answer to her question, she heard someone climbing the bridge ladder, and she scooted into a sitting position with her back against the wall. She stared through the huge windows in the wheelhouse and silhouettes of several people appeared. They moved toward the entrance, and she sucked in her breath in fear. Were these the ones who'd been sent to kill her?

The man who'd abducted her walked into the room first and smiled at her. "You've got company."

He moved aside for the others to enter, and she almost fainted in shock at who appeared.

"Charles? Nora? What are you doing here?"

FOURTEEN

Brad drained the last drop of coffee that Bill had insisted he drink when the door to the office opened, and Bill rushed in. "I just got a call from my agent at the phone company. He's emailing the records. In fact they're probably already here." He sat down at his desk, pulled up his email and smiled. "Here they are."

Brad looked over Bill's shoulder as he opened the message, and his eyes widened when he saw the name. "Josh Nelson was her last caller?"

Bill glanced up. "You know him?"

"Yes, he works at the clinic with Laura." He looked back at the records. "There's no activity after that."

Bill pushed to his feet. "Not on making or receiving calls, but the phone company is tracking which towers her phone hit since the time she left the hospital. My agent will be relaying the information to me as we head out."

"I'll drive," Brad called out as they dashed to the parking lot. "I probably know the city better than you, and you can talk with your agent while I drive."

"Good idea," Bill responded.

They jumped in Brad's car, and he pulled up to the entrance to the street. "Which way do I go?"

"Agent West, we're leaving the field office. Do you have a direction we need to head?" He glanced at Brad. "They've got the information. The last towers are along Highway 51 headed north out of the city. The phone hasn't hit on a tower in nearly an hour. The last one was near the river near an industrial area."

Brad nodded. "I know the area. Now if we can find the position of the phone in the area, maybe we'll find Laura."

Bill pulled out his cell phone and punched in a number. "Maybe there's a way we can find them if they're near the river. I'm calling Harbor Patrol for boats to start a search north of downtown. Maybe they can spot where they're taking her."

"Thanks. Then call Memphis P.D. and have them get the helicopter in the air. Tell them both to look for a black SUV. If we can get the helicopter up and a boat in the water, we should have the area along the river-bank covered."

Bill made the calls, and then sank back against his seat. "That's taken care of. They're on their way."

Brad glanced over at him and saw him biting down on his lip. "Is something wrong?"

"There's something I didn't tell you. That last hit on a tower…"

Brad frowned. "Yes?"

"The phone's activity stopped."

Brad swallowed hard and gripped the steering wheel tighter. "What does that mean?"

"It means that for some reason the phone is no longer in service."

Perspiration popped out on Brad's forehead, and he licked his lips. He hesitated for a moment before he spoke. "She's not dead, Bill. I could feel it if she was. She's not dead."

"I hope not, Brad. I really hope not."

His cell phone rang, and Brad pulled it from its clip to his ear. "Austin."

"Brad, this is Rick Thompson. I have something for you."

He sat up straighter. "What is it?"

"I finally got through all the dead ends and found my way into the dummy corporation. There're all kinds of companies set up, and a lot of people are going to have some explaining to do about why they're partners with Tony Lynch's operation."

"That's great news. Were you able to track Pennington to it?"

"I'm afraid not. It looks like he's clean. Nothing about him anywhere."

Brad shook his head. "There has to be. Maybe you overlooked him."

"No, I didn't. It was another guy, one I'd never heard of. He's the lawyer, and it looks like he's the one running all of Tony's organization now. His name is Charles McKenzie."

"Charles McKenzie?" Brad's hand loosened on the steering wheel, and the car swerved to the shoulder of the road. He pulled back onto the highway and shook his head. "Are you sure?"

"Yeah, he tried to hide, but I found him. Do you know this guy?"

Brad's eyes narrowed. "Yes, and he's been right under our noses for twenty years. Thanks, Rick. Can you get me copies of all your research?"

"I'll have it to you in the morning."

"Thanks, and, Rick..." He paused, hoping this information wasn't too late to help Laura. "I really owe you on this one."

Laura's surprise at seeing Charles and Nora quickly turned to relief. If they had found her, maybe Brad wasn't too far behind and would soon be here. She opened her mouth to ask how they knew where she was when she hesitated. They didn't look shocked to see her, and they were standing very close to the man who'd abducted her.

Before she could speak, Charles turned to the man. "Did everything go as planned, Sam?"

So Sam was his name. But how did Charles know that, and what plan was he talking about?

"Yeah, the kid's wrapped in a tarp downstairs."

"Good."

She heard the words, but they didn't make sense. What kid in a tarp? And then it hit her. They were talking about Josh. His body was wrapped and ready to be dumped in the river. And her abduction was the plan they were talking about.

Laura looked at Nora, the woman she'd loved since she was a child, the one who had shielded her from the sight of her parents' burning bodies the day their car exploded. Then she looked at Charles, the man who'd worked in her father's office, the man her father had trusted. Was it possible she had been so wrong about them? Tears rolled down her face.

There was so much she wanted to know, but she could only voice one word. *"Why?"* She swallowed and tried again. "You were like family to us."

No emotion showed on Nora's face. "Family is very

important to me. My family, that is. And I'm sick and tired of your family trying to tear down everything my family has built."

Laura frowned. "What are you talking about?"

"Tony Lynch," Nora hissed. "He's my uncle, my mother's brother. And he's been good to Charles and me. Your father wanted to bring him down, to break him, to strip him of everything he'd worked for all his life, but we put a stop to that. And then you have to come back to Memphis and start dragging up all those old memories. We couldn't let you get away with that."

Laura strained against her bonds. If she could reach Nora, she would claw her eyes out for the years of deceit. But she felt more than anger. She felt betrayed for all the years she had loved Charles and Nora and thought they felt the same about her and her brother.

Her forehead wrinkled. "How could you pretend all those years to love Mark and me?"

Nora shrugged. "It was something we had to do. I have to admit that the morning of the bombing really was difficult. I should never have let you and Mark go out on the porch to wave goodbye to your parents."

Shock rushed through her, and Laura shook her head as if denying what Nora had just said would erase the words. "You knew about the bomb?" She barely was able to whisper.

Nora glanced at Charles. "Of course I did. Charles planted it on the car the night before, and I kept watch for him. My uncle told us exactly what to do."

Laura's shock turned to contempt, and she curled her lips in disgust. "Your uncle is a monster, Nora. Everything he's accomplished has come about because he took it from someone else. He's a thief, a murderer, a trafficker in human beings, a drug dealer…"

Nora's slap across Laura's face stopped her list of accusations. "You don't know anything. He's a good man who took care of every member of his family."

Laura wrinkled her nose. "Yeah, a family who has the same stench of evil on them that he does. I don't know how I could have been so blind to you."

Charles stepped forward and looked down at her. "Well, it doesn't matter now." He turned to Sam. "Get her on board our boat. It's time for this barge to leave."

Sam reached down, jerked her to her feet and slung her over his shoulder. "Let's go."

Laura sucked in her breath as he walked out of the wheelhouse and began the climb down the ladder. When they reached the deck, he put her down and led her to where Charles and Nora's sleek bow rider sat tied to the tug. She remembered spending the day with them on their boat earlier in the summer. It had been a wonderful day of swimming, fishing and sunbathing. Now it looked as if she might be scheduled for something too horrible to think about.

Sam stepped down into the boat, pulled her after him and shoved her onto one of the padded seats in the bow area. "Sit still, or I'll tie you down."

Charles and Nora climbed into the boat, and Nora settled on the seat beside Laura. "Don't worry, Sam. I'll keep her company. Now you need to tell the captain to get to the wheelhouse and get that barge on the way. The buyers will be waiting in St. Louis for you."

Sam nodded. "Yes, ma'am."

He hopped back up to the tugboat and walked to the cabin underneath the wheelhouse. He knocked, and a man who Laura assumed was the captain stepped outside and climbed the ladder to the upper deck.

When they reached the wheelhouse, Sam waved at Charles. He glanced at Nora. "It looks like everything's under control here. We might as well get started. I know Laura is just *dying* to find out what awaits her."

Nora laughed, and the sound chilled Laura's bones. Charles turned the engine on, and the boat eased away from the side of the tugboat. Once he'd maneuvered into the channel, he pointed the bow north and headed upriver.

Laura glanced back for one last glimpse at the Memphis skyline. In the distance she could see a helicopter flying low along the riverbank. Its rotors flashed in the fading afternoon sun. She watched it a moment before she turned back and faced forward.

Her thoughts went to Brad, and she wondered where he was at that moment. She closed her eyes and said a quick prayer that he wouldn't grieve too much over her death and that he would find happiness in his life.

Then she opened her eyes and took a deep breath to bolster her courage. She would not let Charles and Nora see her fear. Whatever they did to her, she wouldn't give them that pleasure.

Bill's cell phone rang, and he jerked it to his ear. "Diamond." He turned to Brad. "The helicopter has spotted a black SUV at a barge docking station by the river. He's called for officers to respond, and Harbor Patrol is about to pull up."

"Where's the location?"

"They're giving me instructions now." He nodded his head as he listened, stared out the windshield and pointed to a road just ahead. "Turn there. Drive about a mile down to the river."

Brad flipped on the siren and flashing lights and swerved into the left turn lane. He accelerated as the car roared down the road lined with tall trees. He caught a glimpse of the river and then the mainmast of a boat. He skidded to a stop next to a black SUV and drew his gun and badge as he raced toward the tugboat.

Behind him other sirens wailed as additional police officers rushed to the scene. The helicopter hovered overhead, and officers from Harbor Patrol climbed aboard the tug just as he and Bill jumped on board. He heard the other squad cars screech to a halt in the parking area.

The captain and three crewmen ran out of the wheelhouse toward the stern, but their escape was cut off by two officers who jumped in the back of the boat. Two other men, their guns drawn, ran from the cabin underneath the wheelhouse.

Brad aimed his gun at the men and held up his badge. "Police! Drop your guns!"

The larger man muttered a curse, dropped his gun and raised his hands. The other man did the same. Bill motioned to the side of the cabin. "Hands on the wall, with your legs spread."

The other officers appeared with their prisoners, and they lined them up next to the ones facing the cabin. By the time they'd searched and handcuffed the prisoners, three more police squad cars had arrived. A car with two FBI agents pulled to a stop, and they joined the officers swarming aboard the tugboat.

Brad yelled to the arriving officers. "We're looking for a young woman who was abducted in a car like that." He pointed to the SUV sitting nearby. "We have probable cause to believe she may be on board. Spread out and cover every inch of this boat."

One of the officers stepped into the cabin under the wheelhouse but reappeared at the door within seconds. "Detective, there's something wrapped in a tarp in here. I think it's a body."

Brad's legs threatened to collapse, and he reached out for something to steady himself. Bill Diamond grabbed his arm. "I'll go check it out, Brad."

He straightened and shook his head. "No, Bill. I need to see for myself. I'd like it if you'd come with me."

Together they entered the small cabin. He almost changed his mind when he saw the tarp with the ropes tied around it, but he shook his head. If they had killed Laura, he owed it to her to be the one to find her. He dropped to his knees beside the bound body and took a penknife from his pocket. With shaking fingers he cut the rope binding the tarp.

Taking a deep breath, he peeled the cover away from the head and almost collapsed in relief when Josh Nelson's face appeared. He pushed to his feet and stumbled back toward Bill. "It's not her. It's the guy who abducted her. I guess they didn't want to leave any witnesses."

Bill frowned. "Then where is she?"

"I don't know, but I'm going to find out."

Brad strode out the door onto the deck where the prisoners were being guarded by several police officers. "We found a body in there, which puts you all in a lot of trouble. Now we're getting ready to tear this boat apart and see what else you might be hiding. Before we start, does anyone want to tell us anything that might save us some time?"

When no one spoke, he nodded. "I thought that would be your answer." He turned to the officers on board. "Lock these prisoners in the back of the squad cars, then we're going to search this boat."

As the officers led the prisoners away, the captain stopped next to Brad. "You might want to check those containers first. I don't know if the people in there can last much longer."

Brad cast a startled look at the trailers stacked on the barge in front of the tugboat. "There are people in there?"

"Yeah, we were to deliver them to St. Louis."

"Is the woman who was brought aboard in there?"

"No, she's on a boat headed upriver."

Brad grabbed the man's shirt and clenched his fists around the fabric. "Who took her?"

"Charles and his wife. They're going to dump her in the river."

Brad gasped and released the man. "How long have they been gone?"

"They left right before you got here." Brad shoved the man away from him and turned to run toward Bill. "You'll tell the D.A. I helped you, won't you?"

Brad heard the man, but he didn't have time to respond. All he could think about was Laura. Was she still alive, or had Charles and Nora already killed her?

"Bill!" Brad called out as he ran across the deck. "Have them check those trailers first for people inside. Laura's on a boat headed north. I'm off to find her."

"I'll take care of everything here. You go after her."

Brad jumped from the tugboat deck to the Harbor

Patrol boat idling beside it. "We've got to catch an escaping boat," he yelled. "And tell the helicopter we need them, too."

Within minutes they were speeding north up the Mississippi River with the helicopter leading the way. As the sleek Harbor Patrol boat cut through the water, Brad scanned the horizon through a pair of binoculars in hopes of catching a glimpse of the boat.

"How much of a head start do they have?" one of the officers asked him.

"I don't know. Not long I don't think."

"Then they're probably not speeding. If they don't know they're being pursued, they wouldn't want to draw attention to themselves."

"I hope you're right," Brad said.

For the next ten minutes everyone on board was quiet as they sped through the water. Perspiration rolled down Brad's face, but he continued to stare straight ahead through the binoculars. Suddenly a burst of sound crackled over the ship's radio. "Suspect sighted straight ahead. Moving in front to get a better look."

"Was that the helicopter?" he yelled.

The captain nodded as the boat accelerated. He pointed straight ahead. "The helicopter is moving forward."

Brad braced himself to keep from falling as their boat surged forward. He squinted through the binoculars and strained to make out what was happening in the distance. He spotted a white dot on the horizon. It had to be Charles's boat. As he watched, the helicopter dropped down and flew low over the top of Charles's bow rider. Then he climbed in the sky, circled around and flew straight back toward the boat.

The captain laughed and pointed to the maneuver. "Look at that."

He'd barely finished speaking before the helicopter pilot repeated the move over the top and then back across the boat. The Harbor Patrol boat had now moved so close Brad could make out the people in the bow rider.

Charles stood at the wheel, and he could see Nora and Laura sitting in the front of the boat. A wave of relief rushed through him, but he knew she wasn't out of danger yet. They had to get that boat stopped, and Charles appeared determined to not give up.

The Harbor Patrol boat had now moved closer to the bow rider, and the captain spoke into his PA system. "Stop your boat and prepare to be boarded."

The answer from Charles was a bullet that sailed over the top of the boat. Brad gritted his teeth as the bow rider surged forward. "He's ignoring the order."

"Then we'll intercept him."

Brad kept the binoculars trained on the boat as the helicopter made another pass over it and then turned back. This time it dropped lower and barely missed touching the top of the boat.

Beside him, Brad heard the captain mutter to the officer at the helm, "That guy's an idiot. He keeps swerving out of the channel. Doesn't he know there are sandbars all along here?"

The helicopter prepared for another assault, and Brad held his breath. The helicopter flew straight at the boat as if daring Charles to make him move. Brad knew he was too far away for Laura to hear, but he yelled anyway. "Laura, get down!"

As if she'd heard him, Laura lunged forward out of her seat and landed on the deck just as Charles swerved and plowed down the center of a submerged sandbar. Brad watched the impact in horror as Nora's body flew through the air like a rag doll and hit the water on the left side of the boat. Charles landed on the deck amid flying debris that peppered the water as the right side of the boat tore loose. The ship immediately began to take on water as the deck sank into the sandbar. Brad strained for a glimpse of Laura, but he couldn't find her in the wreckage.

The Harbor Patrol boat coasted to a stop next to the wreck, and Brad was over the side before it had stopped. His feet sank into the sand, and the water reached about eighteen inches up his body as he sloshed along the sandbar toward the boat. He pulled his gun, climbed over the end of the boat and came to a stop at the sight in front of him.

Charles faced him with one arm wrapped around Laura's neck and the other holding a gun to her head. Blood ran down the side of his face. "Don't come another step, Brad, or I'll kill her."

Brad held his gun in a two-hand grip and let his gaze move over Laura, from her head to her feet. He didn't see any injuries. "Are you all right?"

"I—I'm fine."

Charles tightened his hold on her. "She won't be if you don't drop that gun."

Brad shook his head. "Charles, you're in a no-win situation here. We know you're the one who's been in charge ever since Tony retired. Before we're through, we'll have enough charges to keep you in prison for the rest of your life. There's no need to add more at this point."

Charles chuckled. "I'm smart enough to recognize I can't escape, but I can sure make your life miserable if I kill your girlfriend before I surrender."

Brad tensed. "You don't want to do that. Let her go." Out of the corner of his eye he caught sight of two officers pulling an injured Nora out of the water. Behind him two more Harbor Patrol officers climbed in. "You're outnumbered here, Charles, and Nora's hurt. She needs a doctor. Release Laura, so we can head back and get Nora to a hospital."

Charles's hand trembled, and he glanced toward where Nora was being lifted into the other boat. "I did everything Tony wanted so I could run the organization. I went to work for Lawrence, then I put the bomb on his car and kept an eye on his kids for years. I thought I had it made. Now everything's gone."

Brad moved closer. "Put the gun down, Charles, and let's go back to Memphis."

He took a deep breath and cocked the trigger of the gun. "No, not until I do this last thing."

Before Brad could move, Laura wiggled in Charles's arms, bent her head down and clamped her teeth into his arm. He yelled, and his grip loosened. With a thrust Laura twisted out of his arms and dropped to the floor. He raised the gun and aimed at her, but Brad fired first.

A surprised look flashed on Charles's face before he dropped the gun and slumped to the floor.

Brad rushed toward Charles and kicked his gun away. He dropped to his knees beside Laura as the other officers took charge of Charles. His fingers fumbled with the ropes that held her prisoner, but he finally pulled her free.

He pulled her into a sitting position and touched her face. "Did they hurt you, Laura?"

She shook her head. "No." Then big tears began to roll down her cheeks. "I was so frightened, Brad. I didn't think you'd find me."

Before he realized what had happened, he had his arms around her, and he had pulled her into a tight embrace. Her arms went around his neck, and he offered up a silent prayer of thanks to God for the blessing of having her back safely.

He put his mouth to her ear and whispered for her alone to hear. "I love you, Laura."

She sighed and pulled away to face him. "I love you, too."

He didn't care how many officers were watching. All he wanted at the moment was to seal their commitment. His lips covered hers, and for the first time in six years he knew what true happiness felt like.

FIFTEEN

A week later Laura sat on the patio of the house she shared with Grace Kincaid and sipped a glass of iced tea. She tipped her head back and let the sun's rays warm her skin. Maybe she was finally beginning to thaw out.

Every time she'd thought about the things that happened last week, an icy feeling crept through her and left her shaking from the cold. She had counseled enough patients who had experienced such feelings, and she always told them they would eventually begin to feel alive again. It was time she took her own advice.

The back door slammed, and Grace emerged carrying a platter of cookies. "I thought these would hit the spot with the tea."

Laura laughed and shook her head. "You've only been home a day, and you've cooked enough food for me that I couldn't possibly eat it all in a month."

Grace dropped down in the chair next to her, and a pout pulled at her mouth. "I can't believe you let this happen to me."

Laura's eyes grew wide. "What are you talking about?"

"I leave town for one week to do a special assignment in England for the station, and you let the biggest story Memphis has ever seen break while I'm gone. That story is one I should have covered."

Laura laughed. "At least you can take credit for getting it started. If you hadn't talked me into doing that interview, Charles never would have sent his goons after me. Maybe the station will let you cover the trials. Brad says there's going to be a lot of them."

Grace straightened in her chair and propped her hands on her hips. "Yeah, and that's another thing I'm upset about. When you came back to Memphis, you made me promise I wouldn't tell him you were in town. Then the minute I'm gone, you run to him at the station."

Laura laughed again. "And that came about because of the men who abducted me after the interview you talked me into doing. So I guess when all is said and done, you're the one to blame for everything that happened."

Grace reached over and grasped Laura's hand. Her face took on a serious look. "I'm glad you can tease about it now. I know it must have been horrible while it was happening. I'm really sorry I wasn't here for you at the time."

Laura squeezed her hand. "Don't worry about it. Everything turned out all right. At least I think it did. Brad told me he loved me after I was rescued, and I told him I loved him, too. Since then, he's been busy tying up the loose ends. He's been by every day, but he's seemed a little remote. He may be having second thoughts about our relationship. Anyway, he's coming over this afternoon and said he wanted to talk to me about something."

Grace glanced at her watch. "I'll be eager to hear what he has to say. I have to go to the station, but I should be back before dinner. Want to order pizza tonight?"

"That sounds good. I'll see you later."

Laura picked up the book she'd brought outside to read and opened it to where she'd left off earlier. She'd only read a few lines when Brad's voice interrupted her. "Would you like some company?"

She closed the book and turned her head as he came out the back door. "I would love some company."

"I met Grace as she was going out. She said for me to come on out here." He sat in the chair next to her and let his gaze drift over her. "How are you feeling today?"

"I'm fine. I talked to Dr. Jones today. I'm going back to work tomorrow. I think I've taken enough time off, and besides they're shorthanded with Josh gone."

She bit down on her lip after she'd spoken. It was still hard to believe that Josh had been working for the people who wanted to kill her.

"I talked to Josh's parents yesterday," Brad said.

"How are they doing?"

"They sounded like they were devastated. Especially the father. They thought they'd lost everything when their house burned, but now they know they really have. Losing their son was the worst thing that could have happened to them, and the fact that he was involved in criminal activities has been the final blow."

Laura's eyes filled with tears. "Josh and his parents aren't the only ones who've been hurt. There are so many more who've suffered because of one man and his crime family. My parents, my brother and me,

Johnny Sherwood, Sylvia Warner, Vince and Melinda Stone, Nathan Carson and his family. And those are just the ones I know about. What about all the people who were sold into slavery, those who bought drugs, the ones who lost all their money in his crooked poker games?" She rubbed her eyes. "There are too many to name."

Brad nodded. "Yes, there are, but there won't be any more people hurt. You helped put a stop to that, and I'm proud of you."

She shook her head. "It was all you, Brad. If you hadn't found me, they wouldn't have been caught."

"But we did find you, and now the men in their organization are in jail. Charles and Nora will be joining them when they're released from the hospital. And there are still a few who have slipped through the cracks, but we'll find them."

For a moment she let her thoughts drift back to the time she'd spent on the barge. The fear she'd felt when she knew she was at the mercy of a group of killers had begun to fade with time, but there was something else that she doubted she would ever be able to erase from her mind—the pitiful sobs and moans she'd heard coming from a storage container. "What happened to the people who were rescued from slavery?"

"Bill called Immigration, and they came and took control of them. The first thing they did was feed them and take care of their medical needs. They're all being returned to their home countries since they were in this country illegally. Most of them were glad to be going home."

Laura gave a contented sigh. "It seems like things are working out well. I went by the hospital today to see Nathan Carson. He was sitting up in bed talking with his wife. I couldn't believe how much progress he's made in a week. He told me he's going to testify about the undercover policeman's death."

"Yes. The D.A. has offered him a deal dropping the charges against him in exchange for his testimony. Now with all of the Lynch mob in jail, we don't think it will be necessary for the Carsons to enter the witness protection program."

Laura pushed to her feet and stretched. "It seems like everybody is having a happy ending."

Brad stood and stared into her eyes. "What about us, Laura? Do we have a happy ending?"

Her breath caught in her throat, and she tried to swallow. "I hope we can, Brad."

He took her hand in his. "I haven't been able to sleep much this past week. I keep waking up with perspiration pouring off me and my body shaking. I can't forget how scared I was when I realized you'd been abducted from the hospital right under my nose. I'm sorry I failed you, Laura."

She reached up and stroked his cheek. "You didn't fail me, Brad. I made the mistake. I should have told you where I was going. You did everything in your power to find me, and you did. I thought I was going to die, and I kept praying for you and for my family."

He tilted his head to one side. "Why were you praying for me?"

"Because I knew how scared and how guilty you'd feel if I was killed, and I prayed that you wouldn't grieve for me and that you would have a happy life."

His eyes darkened, and his arm slid around her waist. "I've known for fifteen years I'd never have a happy life if I wasn't with you. I fell in love with you in the hall in front of our freshman English classroom door, and I've loved you ever since."

"I remember that day. I thought you were the handsomest boy I'd ever seen." She closed her eyes and shook her head. "But we grew up, and I made some mistakes in our relationship, Brad. I should have done things differently instead of leaving and cutting myself off from you. I thought I was doing the right thing at the time. I'm so sorry for hurting you, because I ended up hurting myself more. I've always loved you."

He wrapped both his arms around her and pulled her closer. "Let's put the past where it belongs and concentrate on what lies ahead for us. I don't want to spend another day without things settled between us. So I want to ask you something I asked you a long time ago. Will you marry me?"

She slipped her arms around his neck and pulled his lips close. "I will, and I promise I'll spend the rest of my life making you happy."

His lips covered hers, and the same thrill she'd felt years before when he kissed her returned. After a moment he released her. "I have something for you." He reached into his pocket and pulled out a ring box. "This is for you."

She took it from him and opened the box. Her eyes grew wide as she stared at the ring inside. With tears rolling down her cheeks she looked up at him. "This is the ring you bought for me when we were in college. I can't believe you've kept it."

He nodded. "You gave it back to me when you left. But do you remember what I told you?"

"You said 'I'll put it away for future use.' I thought

you meant you'd give it to the next woman you fell in love with."

He shook his head. "No, I meant I'd keep it to give to you when you came back to me." He pulled the ring from the box and slipped it on her finger. "Now you're back, and the ring is where it was meant to be."

She smiled up at him. "I love you, Brad, and I'm where I was meant to be, too—right here in your arms."

* * * * *

Dear Reader,

Statistics tell us that even in this age of DNA analysis and other technical advances the number of unsolved murder cases each year in the United States continues to grow. Many of these become cold cases, and families are left without answers. Concern for those who are experiencing this problem led me to write the story you have just read. I hope you enjoyed Laura and Brad's journey as they searched for the killers of her parents. It is my prayer that the stories I write and the characters I create will not only entertain you but will also remind you that even when we don't understand the problems we encounter in our lives, God stands ready to offer comfort and peace.

Sandra Robbins

Questions for Discussion

1. In the story, Brad still suffered because Laura had broken their engagement. Have you ever had someone you love hurt you deeply? How did you respond?

2. Although Laura tried to move on with her life, she was still haunted by the images of her parents' deaths. Have you ever been so consumed with grief that it controlled your entire life?

3. Laura tried to distance herself from Memphis, where she'd grown up, but she was drawn back to the city. How did the town where you grew up influence your life?

4. Laura counseled families of crime victims to be aware of their surroundings. When she didn't heed her own advice, she was abducted from the hospital parking lot. Why is it difficult sometimes for individuals to ignore what they know is the right thing to do?

5. The murder of Laura's parents had gone unsolved for nearly twenty years. Have you ever known anyone who lived with the unsolved murder of a relative? How did you minister to that person?

6. What can you do as an individual to bring hope to the families of victims of unsolved crimes?

7. Brad had directed his anger at Laura toward God and thought God had no time for him. Have you ever felt that way?

8. It took the innocent words of a child to open Brad's eyes to God's love. What did Jesus have to say about children?

9. Laura found out she should never have trusted Charles and Nora. Have you ever been deceived by someone you trusted?

10. Brad and Laura decided to put the past behind them and face the future together. Are there problems in your life because of unresolved issues in the past? How can you help to resolve these problems?

REQUEST YOUR FREE BOOKS!

2 FREE RIVETING INSPIRATIONAL NOVELS
PLUS 2 FREE MYSTERY GIFTS

Love Inspired®
SUSPENSE

YES! Please send me 2 FREE Love Inspired® Suspense novels and my 2 FREE mystery gifts (gifts are worth about $10). After receiving them, if I don't wish to receive any more books, I can return the shipping statement marked "cancel." If I don't cancel, I will receive 4 brand-new novels every month and be billed just $4.74 per book in the U.S. or $5.24 per book in Canada. That's a savings of at least 21% off the cover price. It's quite a bargain! Shipping and handling is just 50¢ per book in the U.S. and 75¢ per book in Canada.* I understand that accepting the 2 free books and gifts places me under no obligation to buy anything. I can always return a shipment and cancel at any time. Even if I never buy another book, the two free books and gifts are mine to keep forever.

123/323 IDN F5AC

Name	(PLEASE PRINT)	
Address		Apt. #
City	State/Prov.	Zip/Postal Code

Signature (if under 18, a parent or guardian must sign)

Mail to the **Harlequin® Reader Service:**
IN U.S.A.: P.O. Box 1867, Buffalo, NY 14240-1867
IN CANADA: P.O. Box 609, Fort Erie, Ontario L2A 5X3

**Are you a current subscriber to Love Inspired Suspense books
and want to receive the larger-print edition?
Call 1-800-873-8635 or visit www.ReaderService.com.**

* Terms and prices subject to change without notice. Prices do not include applicable taxes. Sales tax applicable in N.Y. Canadian residents will be charged applicable taxes. Offer not valid in Quebec. This offer is limited to one order per household. Not valid for current subscribers to Love Inspired Suspense books. All orders subject to credit approval. Credit or debit balances in a customer's account(s) may be offset by any other outstanding balance owed by or to the customer. Please allow 4 to 6 weeks for delivery. Offer available while quantities last.

Your Privacy—The Harlequin® Reader Service is committed to protecting your privacy. Our Privacy Policy is available online at www.ReaderService.com or upon request from the Harlequin Reader Service.
We make a portion of our mailing list available to reputable third parties that offer products we believe may interest you. If you prefer that we not exchange your name with third parties, or if you wish to clarify or modify your communication preferences, please visit us at www.ReaderService.com/consumerchoice or write to us at Harlequin Reader Service Preference Service, P.O. Box 9062, Buffalo, NY 14269. Include your complete name and address.

LIS13R

SPECIAL EXCERPT FROM

Love Inspired.
SUSPENSE

*Photojournalist Gabriel Murdock always gets the best
shot but when he's banished to New Orleans to cover a
"fluff" piece about an American widowed princess, he
is not happy. When the beautiful Lara Kincade is put in
danger, Gabriel smells a real story brewing underneath
her polished, polite exterior. Read on for a sneak peek at
IN PURSUIT OF A PRINCESS by Lenora Worth,
available September 2013 from
Harlequin Love Inspired Suspense.*

"No. They said I'd have to go to a hospital to be tested. I
can't do that. The press would swarm the place."

"And whoever poisoned you could easily find you."
Gabriel shook his head. "I'm trying to keep you safe without
overstepping the boundaries."

Her smile was real this time. "You're a gallant man."

He exhaled a breath. "I'm not that gallant. I'm chasing a story.
But I will honor my obligations to our original agreement."

"Of course you will." She shouldn't feel so disappointed
that he didn't declare he'd protect her no matter the challenge.
After all, the man was here to do a job. And she obviously
didn't have any business thinking of him in any other way.
Especially not in a "please grab me and hold me in your arms"
way. After the story he'd told her of the beautiful Adina, was it
any wonder the man didn't want to get emotionally involved?

He finally touched a finger to her right arm, the brush of
his nearness rasping across her hot skin like a warm kiss.
"Lara, you know I'd do anything for you."

She could only nod. She didn't know anything anymore. "I

hear something else in your declaration."

He shuffled his feet, lifted his hand away. "I want to help you. I…admire you and your work here and I get how important it is that you finish what your husband started. But some things are too costly to continue."

Falling for him would certainly come at a high cost.

She swallowed. "I want to continue because I have to keep moving, Gabriel. I…I've stayed busy since the day they buried my husband. I have to do this, for him."

"For him, Lara?"

A single tear slid down her face. She should tell Gabriel everything….

Don't miss IN PURSUIT OF A PRINCESS
by Lenora Worth, available September 2013 from
Harlequin Love Inspired Suspense.

Love Inspired
SUSPENSE
RIVETING INSPIRATIONAL ROMANCE

SEAL UNDER SIEGE
by
Liz Johnson

Navy SEAL Tristan Sawyer rescued Staci Hayes, but the
missionary still isn't safe. With the bombing plot she overheard,
she and Tristan race to stop the terrorists before the naval base
goes up in smoke.

MEN of VALOR

Available September 2013
wherever Love Inspired Suspense books are sold.

www.LoveInspiredBooks.com

LIS44554

A FATHER'S PROMISE
by
CAROLYNE AARSEN

When the child she gave up for adoption shows up in
town with her adoptive father, Renee must overcome
her guilt to find true love.

Available September 2013
wherever Love Inspired books are sold.